They were alone; now was the time she had been waiting for.

Jenny closed the door on her father's retreating figure, then turned to face Clint, her mind busily searching for the right way to approach him.

"You're very protective of him, aren't you?" Clint asked.

"Yes, I suppose I am," she replied, crossing to the fireplace to warm herself. "You see, my mother died when I was born, so we have only each other. But what about your family?" she asked curiously. "You've never told us anything about yourself."

"There's not a lot to tell," he replied. The tone was intended to be casual, but Jenny had not missed the subtle tightening of his mouth as he spoke. "I'm just a drifter, like a lot of other guys wandering around Cripple Creek."

"No, you aren't just another drifter, Clint Kincaid." Her tone was softly compelling. "And you aren't like the other men who are wandering around out there."

Jenny walked over to the sofa and stared down at him. "Who are you?" she asked. "Where do you come from?"

KINCAID OF CRIPPLE CREEK

Peggy Darty

Serenade/Saga
BOOKS
of the Zondervan Publishing House
Grand Rapids, Michigan

A Note From the Author:

I love to hear from my readers! You may correspond with me by writing:

>Peggy Darty
>1415 Lake Drive S.E.
>Grand Rapids, MI 49506

KINCAID OF CRIPPLE CREEK
Copyright 1985 by The Zondervan Corporation

Serenade Saga is an imprint of
The Zondervan Publishing House
1415 Lake Drive, S.E.
Grand Rapids, Michigan 49506

ISBN 0-310-46982-1

Edited by Anne Severance
Designed by Kim Koning

Printed in the United States of America

85 86 87 88 89 90 / 10 9 8 7 6 5 4 3 2 1

For my mother

CHAPTER 1

JENNIFER TOWNLEY PAUSED on the doorstep of her two-room cabin, buttoning her navy woolen cloak against the piercing cold. A raw wind raced across the hard-packed snow, snatching at her long dark skirt and ruffling thick black hair about a delicate oval face.

She shivered into her cloak, longing to return to the warmth of her kitchen, yet needing to borrow flour to finish her baking. As if to fortify herself for the short trek to her neighbor's home, she turned wide-set violet eyes toward the distant Sangre de Cristos.

Sangre de Cristos—the blood of Christ. The early Spanish explorers had named the mountains well, Jennifer thought, watching the effect of the late-afternoon sun striking the snow-capped peaks. The rosy hue never failed to remind her of the sacrificial blood of Christ, a thought that inspired her with strength and gave her the sense that any sacrifice she might make here in this strange new land was paltry by comparison.

In jarring contrast to that peaceful scene was the town below her. Her gaze fell to the cluster of flimsy pine buildings fronted by rough, uneven streets: Cripple Creek. Like the volcanic eruption that had tortured the earth centuries before, the settlement reflected tumbled disorder. The gulches and hills that had once been trodden by restless cattle were disrupted now by a new upheaval—the search for gold. Men scratched and dug into the earth with fevered persistence, hoping that 1894 would be the year they found the magical vein of ore that would transport them from rags to riches. Hadn't it already happened to a fortunate few?

Another blast of wind shook her slim frame and she hurried across the tiny patch of yard to Maude Jacobs' cabin.

At ten thousand feet everything seemed more intense—the wind, the sun, the rain, the snow. Jennifer had seen the ravages of the high country on the faces of other young women, making them old before their time. Though there were yet no creases about her dark-fringed eyes, and no wrinkles marring the smoothness of her high brow, she knew the years ahead would likely carve themselves into her countenance as well.

She reached Maude's step and paused to rake away the snow that clung to the soles of her boots. She gave a small sigh, dismissing her irritation with the weather and the toll it demanded. It was fruitless to fuss over matters one could not control.

Squaring her shoulders, she lifted a small hand to tap softly on Maude's plank door, glancing at the vertical boards of the cabin lined with wooden strips. All the wind-whipped cabins around her were similar, and rented for fifteen to twenty dollars a month—an absurd price even for a dwelling back in St. Louis. *But I left St. Louis behind six months ago* , she reminded herself. This was her new home and she would accept it as she found it. If nineteen years had taught her nothing else, they had taught her how to achieve a quiet balance between want and plenty.

A heavy tread jarred the cabin before the door swung back, and the aroma of cinnamon and cloves brought a sudden hunger pang to Jennifer's empty stomach.

"Jenny Townley! What are you doing out in this cold?" Maude scolded, a good-natured grin creasing her round face.

Although Maude was at least three and a half inches taller than Jenny, and outweighed her by fifty pounds, Jenny had soon learned not to be intimidated by the older woman's aggressive manner. She knew that beneath the life-lined face and strong body, a sweet spirit ached to pour out the love of her childless years.

"I came to borrow some flour—if you have extra," Jenny added quickly. "We had unexpected company and—"

"Company!" Maude yanked the young woman's arm and pulled her inside, slamming the door against the howling March wind. "Yore pa is going to *company* you right into starvation! Who was you feedin' this time?" Maude asked, wiping floured hands on her muslin apron.

"There were members from the congregation over for coffee and cake yesterday," she sighed, "and last night an elderly man came looking for a place to sleep. I never know *who* is coming, but I've learned to keep a cake in the cupboard."

9

It was common knowledge that Joseph Townley, the minister from St. Louis, had a reputation for caring. Perhaps her father cared too much, Jennifer sometimes thought, but they couldn't turn a needy soul from their door when this was part of their very reason for being here. Her father's heart-stirring messages, delivered to a small crowd in the rear of the grocery store on Sunday mornings, were followed by lengthy discussions around their dining table, where Jenny served as her father's hostess. And through the week there were always people in need, rough desperate miners whose lives were being changed by the Bibles her father gave them.

"It appears to me you need a rest," Maude called, lumbering to the far end of the room which served as the kitchen. "You and yore pa ought to stop worryin' about all them drifters who'll sponge off anybody who'll feed 'em." She gave a brisk nod to emphasize her words, tucking a coarse strand of gray hair back into the bun at the nape of her neck. "My Ed says there's an average of twenty folks a day comin' into the territory—tenderfeet who toss dynamite around like it was a stick of hard candy. Ever since Bob Womack yelled 'gold' the word's spread like a brushfire."

Jenny nodded, thinking about the many wagons rolling down the hillside beyond her door that bore familiar, crudely lettered signs on their canvas sides: "Goin' to Cripple Creek!"

"I know," she smiled, "but every time I see another wagon, I wonder about the people inside. Who are they? How far have they come?" *And will their dreams come true here?* she thought to herself, *or will they lose everything?* "There are a few people who have struck it rich, though," her voice lifted encouragingly. "Look at Mr. Stratton, for example."

"Yeah, but there aren't many like him." Maude marched across the room, extending a tin cup filled with flour. "You can't feed 'em all, honey."

"I know, Maude, but Father says you can't outgive God. And He's been so good to us. Well, thanks for the flour." Jenny stood, mentally bracing herself to face the bitter cold outside the door. "We'll have some money coming in soon . . ." she faltered, wondering if there would be enough to meet their needs. They just might "company" themselves into starvation, after all. Although her father tried to conceal the fact of their dwindling funds, Jenny had already perceived the truth.

"Jenny!" Maude's voice halted her at the door. "Honey, you need to find yourself a nice young man, a man of means." The tired blue eyes took on a youthful twinkle. "Someone who'd buy you a fine home, dress you in style." She scowled at Jenny's plain worn skirt.

A tender smile touched Jenny's lips as she looked into the woman's sympathetic face. What Maude lacked in grace and refinement, she more than made up in genuine love and charity.

"Maude, I appreciate your concern," she replied, "but I'm happy. *Really*, I am!"

"Phooey! You're just like your pa!" Maude wagged her head in exasperation. "Well, get some rest, you hear?"

Jenny waved, and lowered her head against the biting wind. As the heels of her boots made crunching sounds in the deep snow, she considered Maude's well-meaning advice. Was she just like her pa—or her

11

ma? Her smooth brow puckered thoughtfully. She had never known the lovely dark-haired Ella Townley who had died giving her birth. Relatives spoke fondly of her mother, describing her as a beautiful woman with a kind and loving spirit.

Unexpectedly tears sprang to her deep violet eyes, blurring the snowy path. A poignant loneliness settled over her—as heavy and cold as the winter day. If only she could have known her mother, the wonderful woman her father still loved and missed after all these years.

She sighed, the cheerful mask she had presented to Maude slipping a little. It was this dreary weather that had prompted her melancholy, she told herself, and the strain of company and meals. And . . . what else?

In her childhood years, she had sensed a void in her young life, a void that only a mother could fill, despite aunts who showered her with affection and a father who loved her dearly. Still . . . another kind of loneliness had crept in recently to stake its claim on her heart—the kind of loneliness that stung when she saw other women walking along the streets with their husbands, or bouncing children on their knees.

Thrusting those thoughts aside, she scraped her boots against the slab step of her cabin. She couldn't imagine herself in any other role. Here in this remote mining town, she and her father had found a ministry that left them challenged—even exhausted—yet deeply rewarded. Her moments of melancholy were usually short-lived.

Entering the warmth of her cabin, Jenny paused to regard with renewed appreciation the Chippendale sofa and chair, vivid contrast to Maude's handcrafted pieces. Her father had brought the elegant furnishings with them on the wagon, and they were a source of comfort to her, a tangible legacy of the life she had left behind.

Joseph Townley, seated at the kitchen table, glanced up from the scribbled notes for his Sunday sermon. Laying his pen aside, he flexed his calloused fingers and looked up at his daughter, who was removing her cloak and hanging it on the wooden hook by the door.

Jenny smiled warmly at her father, and did not realize the picture she made as she did so. Thick black hair, as black as a raven's wing, framed a pale ivory face—a face that had drawn more than one open stare from men on the streets.

She hurried across the room, her long skirt swishing over the rag rug that covered the boarded floors. Jenny's every movement reflected purpose and direction. *So like your mother*, her father had often told her.

"Father, why so serious?" Jenny asked, catching his searching gaze upon her.

Joseph raked a bony hand through sparse dark hair. "I'm thinking that you belong in some refined girl's school back East," he answered on a heavy sigh. "And I'm wondering what your mother would think about my bringing you to this uncivilized place!"

Jenny set the cup of flour on a shelf, then hurried over to lay a gentle hand on her father's shoulder. "You know this is where I want to be. Why, these past months have been the most exciting of my entire life!"

"It's been a hard winter." He shook his head. Jenny knew his worry went beyond the cold and blustery months they had spent in the cabin. His real concern lay with the boom town below them. Soon that night the electric arc lights would blaze, piano music would fill the saloons, and ladies of the night would stand in doorways, beckoning. And if a miner had any money left after the saloons and the women, the gambling tables would take the remainder of his hard-earned cash.

"I'm troubled for these poor souls who come in from the diggin's only to be fleeced of their last cent," he admitted sadly.

"And then someone will tell them about *you*." Jenny's eyes glowed with pride and affection. "And of course you'll help them."

A hammering on their door brought Joseph to his feet, the old concern lining his face again. When he opened the door, a red-bearded giant of a man stood before them.

"Mr. Benson!" Her father's voice was filled with warm welcome. "Please come in. Jenny," he called over his shoulder, "fresh coffee, please, dear."

"I invited a friend from the diggin's to come along." The bearded man spoke in a sharp, matter-of-fact tone.

"He's welcome, of course. . . . I met Mr. Benson on the street yesterday," he explained to Jenny. "He's come all the way from St. Looey."

Jenny cast a surreptitious glance at the man as she pumped water into the smoke-stained coffeepot. Bloodshot eyes encased in puffy flesh seemed to attack her, crawling up and down her simple clothes, taking in every detail. The blood shot to her cheeks, quickly warming her face, as she whirled back to the coffee. He was obviously no gentlemen! But this was not the first time she had encountered an evil leer in a town where men outnumbered women ten to one.

14

As the frigid air continued to fill the cabin, she turned toward the open door, her eyes widening in surprise.

There she saw the other man, tugging at the reins of a prancing, fawn-colored stallion. Jenny's breath caught in her throat, and in that first swift yet powerful impression, she knew immediately she had never met a man like this one.

He sat tall in the saddle, thick golden hair, lean chiseled features, bold blue eyes—as majestic as the rugged beauty of the mountains in the distance. Sheer masculine power emanated from both man and stallion with an effect that seemed to immobilize Joseph Townley as well.

"Clint, here's the man I was tellin' you about," Benson yelled to the rider. "Reverend Townley, Clint Kincaid. Kincaid works the claim next to mine," he explained.

Clint Kincaid nodded, swinging a long leg over his saddle and easing his tall frame to the ground. His buckskin jacket strained against well-toned muscles of shoulder and chest as he tethered his horse to a hitching rail sheltered from the wind. Once in the doorway, he turned to Joseph Townley, his hand outstretched.

"It's an honor to meet you, sir." The voice was deep, rich, pleasant to the ear.

Jenny's gaze dropped to the large suntanned hand, clasping her father's in a brisk handshake.

"I'm happy to make your acquaintance, Mr. Kincaid. Come in! Come in!" Joseph stepped aside and shut the door behind them. "This is my daughter, Jennifer."

Jenny acknowledged the introduction with a smile

and a fleeting glance. Then her dark lashes fluttered in the embarrassing shyness that often overwhelmed her in the presence of men. For the hundredth time, she wished with all of her heart that she were not so shy.

"How do you do?" she murmured softly.

She had expected a polite nod, a brief response—anything but the intense gaze that held hers as he strolled across the room.

Wordlessly he clasped her small hand, and for one second that seemed to stretch into eternity, he merely stared. Then the chiseled lips parted and white teeth flashed in a wide smile.

"Miss Jennifer Townley . . ."

He released her hand, the golden head dipping in a perfunctory bow. In that moment, Jenny considered Clint Kincaid the epitome of culture and refinement—a rare combination in a camp where men spat tobacco juice on the board sidewalks and drunken cowboys brawled in the dusty streets.

He stepped back then, facing the men, and she stared after him, her heart racing. Confused, unable to think straight, she turned back to the cookstove, trying to remember what she was about to do.

Just as she drew a deep breath to calm her nerves, Benson's presumptuous words jerked her back to reality.

"Thought we'd take supper with you, Reverend—if it's not too much trouble!"

"Oh no," Clint interrupted quickly. "I wouldn't think of intruding!"

"No intrusion, is it Jenny? Whatever we have is yours," her father insisted, bridging the awkward moment with his usual grace.

Jenny glanced at her mixing bowl and flour, to the

still unfinished cake. Supper! She had planned on reheating the small portion of stew left over from yesterday, but that meager amount would never stretch to feed three hungry men. And she couldn't ask Maude for another handout.

Booted feet jarred the planked floor as the men crossed to the small stone fireplace to warm themselves. With their presence, the musky scent of leather and horse flesh drifted through the close quarters, mingling with the familiar smells of coffee and woodsmoke. Jenny longed for her vanishing lilac sachet to sweeten the strong aroma of a man's world.

She glanced back at her father's pleasant face. No doubt, he would sacrifice his own food if the supper ran low. Why couldn't she be as strong as he? And hadn't the Lord met their needs thus far? Her gaze dropped to the curl of steam rising from the coffeepot. Coffee, the most important staple for Colorado winters, had been given them by a generous member of the congregation. Not everyone had an outstretched hand!

Seizing her bleached muslin apron from its hook, she pulled it over her dark hair, tying the narrow strings about her waist. Somehow, *somehow*, she would get through this meal, she told herself. Reaching for a hair ribbon, she whisked her hair back from her face and secured the scarlet ribbon around the thick coil at the base of her neck.

She stole a glance toward the living room and was startled to find Clint Kincaid appraising her again. She forced herself to turn away, wandering to her shelf of skillets in an effort to ignore his watchful gaze.

She thought about this handsome stranger as she lifted a heavy skillet and placed it on the wood-burning stove. Unlike Benson, the expression on his face was neither bold nor disrespectful. In contrast, a look of tenderness, even concern, filled the perceptive blue eyes—a deep, rich blue, like the Colorado sky.

She stared at the skillet, wondering what she had intended to put in it. Checking her supplies, she came upon her seasoning pork, an unopened tin of molasses, and five potatoes reposing in a darkened corner of the shelf under the cast-iron skillet. And there was Maude's flour, she realized with relief. She could make biscuits with the flour and worry about a cake tomorrow. She would simply prepare what she had and hope for the best.

She stole another peek toward the fireplace where the men stood talking with her father.

The balding, red-bearded fellow was at least six feet tall, hands like hams, a heavy paunch hanging over the belt of his dusty trousers that were patched at the knee. In contrast, Clint Kincaid's jeans were neat, unpatched, and his long legs were thrust into brown leather boots, the soles scraped free of snow. Benson, she saw regrettably, had trailed a puddle of water across her clean floor!

"Not one vein of ore!" Benson roared. "My life savings shot to hell! Er, beg pardon, Reverend. But I never should of left St. Looey!"

"What about you, Mr. Kincaid?" Her father turned to the man leaning against the mantel, staring thoughtfully into the flames that licked at the thick aspen logs before devouring them in a blaze.

"My claim looks promising," he shrugged, "but it's too soon to tell."

Jenny turned back to her biscuit dough, thoughtfully kneading it on the floured board. From the periphery of her vision, she caught the golden-haired stranger watching her again. He was a man of few words, she thought, and recalling the sudden reserve in his tone when he spoke of his mining claim, Jenny sensed that he was a private person. Strange. He and his swaggering neighbor were an unlikely pair.

Damp ringlets fell over her forehead as she worked, and the heat of the stove turned her cheeks a rosy pink. Hurriedly she poured the coffee into thick mugs and placed them on a tray.

As she passed the tray around, Benson's fat hand shot out greedily. He grunted in satisfaction. Jenny averted her gaze to the mug, noticing his dirt-encrusted nails, and turned next to the tall stranger.

"Thank you, ma'am." His voice was smooth, deep-timbered, respectful. Her eyes crept to his tanned face and lingered as she tentatively returned his smile.

"Thank you, Jenny." Joseph Townley's voice penetrated the spell, and she turned to hand him his coffee. "When are you gentlemen heading back to camp?" he asked.

Kincaid did not reply. He merely sipped his coffee and studied Benson over the rim of his cup.

Benson's beady eyes darkened above the red beard as he gulped down the hot coffee. "Tonight!" he shouted. "Luck's bound to change."

Jenny turned back to the kitchen, irritated by Benson's manner. Still, if her father had invited him to their home, she must be civil.

Quickly, she set the tin plates around the small pine table, which was covered with her best lace cloth. The cloth seemed dramatically out of place here, but her intuition told her that Clint Kincaid would appreciate quality.

When finally the table was set and the food ready to serve, she announced supper.

"Aren't you joining us, Jenny?" her father asked, glancing at the three plates.

"No, not just yet." She shook her head and hurried back to the stove. She found surprisingly that she had no appetite at all. In fact, the idea of sitting across from the tall stranger and the repugnant Benson twisted her stomach in a spasm of nerves.

Chairs scraped the floor as the men seated themselves, and her father who, perceptively, had not pressed Jenny to join them, offered grace. From her position at the stove, she stole a shuttered glance toward the men. Clint's golden head was lowered respectfully; Benson was glowering at the food.

When the prayer ended, the clatter of knives on tin plates filled the small cabin. Her father spoke of other miners who had discovered gold on their claims, and inspired a cheerful atmosphere over the simple meal.

Jenny busied herself tidying up the kitchen, and soon the pleasant mood lifted her doubtful spirits. Amazingly, she had managed to produce a meal that was being devoured with apparent enjoyment.

Thank you, Lord, she prayed silently. To her amazement, their meager supply of food had provided a sufficient meal.

"Where is your home, Mr. Kincaid?" her father inquired.

"Colorado," he replied, suddenly studying his plate.

There was no further explanation, and the mystique that Jenny already felt surrounding this man deepened. He seemed so reluctant to talk about himself, and for one who appeared to be a natural born-charmer, she found his reserve tantalizing.

"I see," her father replied, pushing his chair back from the table. "Well, Joe Warren at the grocery store has asked me to deliver supplies to the mining sites." He turned to his daughter and offered, "Jenny, maybe you'd like to come with me."

"Begging your pardon, sir," Clint spoke up, "but I don't think you'd want to bring your daughter around the mining sites. It's no place for a lady!"

Jenny whirled with a frown. She thought his statement made her father sound naive, or even worse, negligent. She sauntered over to stand beside her father's chair.

"I'm not afraid!" she declared, her violet eyes darting a challenge.

Clint regarded her with a wry grin. "Mining areas are unsafe for anyone, ma'am," he said, his tone softening, "but particularly for a beautiful lady."

Before Jenny could respond she felt Benson's beady eyes upon her, and she glanced quickly in his direction. She was confronted with a wicked smile.

How dare Benson sit at their table, eat their food, then smirk at her in a vulgar manner! Jenny was seething, and gave him a scathing glare. Then she turned to her father.

"I'm a bit tired," she said. "Will you excuse me?"

Her father sat quietly studying Benson, and for a fleeting second, Jenny saw unspoken communication flashing between them. Apparently he had seen Benson's leering as well. Her father said nothing, but a message was delivered nonetheless.

Benson shuffled uncomfortably, his eyes dropping quickly to his plate.

"Yes, of course," her father replied turning to Jenny.

She hurried to her room, and quickly shut the door behind her. Benson was lecherous, of that she was certain. And her protective father undoubtedly perceived that as well.

A relieved sigh slipped from her lips as she slowly stretched her weary body onto the bed. He wouldn't be invited back to their home, she decided, recalling the set of her father's jaw.

Chairs were being moved about as booted footsteps resounded across the floor. Her father's voice rose above the others, bidding the men good night.

They were leaving! Jenny was eager to get Benson out of the house, but then she remembered Clint . . . her heart sank.

"Please tell your daughter that I enjoyed her meal." Clint's deep voice echoed through the cabin.

Jenny's heart leaped. She entertained thoughts of returning to the living room, but that would be awkward after her dramatic exit.

She hugged her feather pillow against her, a terrible sadness engulfing her.

Will I ever see Clint Kincaid again? she wondered, as hoof-beats tapped out a trail on the snowy road beyond their door.

Clint Kincaid, she murmured to herself, staring through her tiny window to the dark, cloudless sky.

Jenny felt as though she had just closed her eyes when her father's urgent voice jolted her awake. She vaguely remembered washing the supper dishes and dressing for bed. Could it be morning?

"Jenny. *Jenny!* Wake up!"

Jenny pushed herself up on one elbow, and blinked at the silhouette of her father outlined in the narrow doorway by the lamp in the kitchen.

"What is it?" she asked thickly. "What's wrong?"

"Get your robe on and come into the kitchen. I need your help."

"Help?"

Flinging the covers back, her bare toes quickly sought the rag rug beside her bed.

"Who's here?" she whispered, shivering, and aware now of shuffling feet in the next room.

"Remember the man who came for supper? Clint Kincaid? He's been shot! They've brought him to us."

Jenny stared wide-eyed as her father bent over the kerosene lantern on her nightstand, igniting its flare.

She blinked, wondering if this were a nightmare or if she were really awake.

"Hurry!" her father urged.

She watched him slip out of her room and close the door. The flicker of the lantern made strange leaping shadows around her, and suddenly her heart thudded against her rib cage as the frightening words he had spoken penetrated her consciousness.

Kincaid . . . *shot!* And they had brought him to her house!

CHAPTER 2

JENNY SCRAMBLED FOR HER ROBE. She pushed the mass of dark hair from her face and fumbled along the top of the bureau for her hair ribbon as the low murmur of voices reached her from the living room.

Panic raced through her as she tossed her hair back and tied the ribbon around it. Part of her was still numb with shock as she hurried to the washstand and poured the pitcher of water into the basin. The splash of cold water that made her cheeks tingle seemed to jar her brain as well, and her thoughts began to flow more coherently as she dried her face on the towel. She opened the door and peered into the living room.

Her father and an older man were bent over Clint. All she could see of his form were the motionless, dark-trousered legs stretched out on a pallet before the fire.

Is he dead? she wondered wildly, moving to her father's side.

"Father, what happened?" She nudged him gently, peering over his shoulder for a glimpse of Clint.

"We found him out back of the Lucky Dollar," said a thin bearded man. "I'm a bartender there." His last comment was mumbled almost apologetically.

But the words struck Jenny like flintstones, and her heart sank within her. The Lucky Dollar was rumored to be the most notorious saloon in Cripple Creek! Had Clint really left their home and gone there? And was he with Benson?

She was conscious of a movement behind her, and she whirled to see another man standing by the door, twirling the wide brim of his black felt hat in dirty hands. She did not know him, but he shuffled uncomfortably when her eyes met his.

"The doc got the bullet out," the bartender whispered, "but he's lost lots of blood. He asked for you, Reverend. That's why we brought him here— what with the hospital overcrowded and all."

Jenny turned back to the pallet, her eyes widening in horror as she looked down into the still face of the man who, only hours earlier, had sat at their table, and beguiled her with his charm.

The firelight played over his bearded face, softening the sunken eyes and slack jaw. His thick golden hair was swept back from his face to reveal a high forehead, lightly creased with lines. He suddenly appeared older than she had thought earlier. He was at least twenty-eight, possibly thirty. The thick beard that covered his face seemed to conceal his true identity, and without the vividness of those intense blue eyes, the face was empty and sad, like a house with no windows.

"We're glad you brought Clint here." Joseph turned to the man offering a reassuring smile.

"What should we do for him?" Jenny asked helplessly.

"The doc said he's gonna come up and check on him in the morning." The man fidgeted. "I reckon all you can do for now is just keep him comfortable."

"Yes, yes, of course we will," Joseph nodded, following the man to the front door.

Jenny dropped to her knees, her worried eyes roaming Clint's lean frame. His coat had been removed, and his other clothing was circled with stains of snow and blood. The red shirt was torn away from the wound, and a thick white bandage covered his chest and right shoulder. It looked like the bullet had narrowly missed his heart!

God works in mysterious ways, she thought, bewildered. She had prayed for the Lord to let her see Clint Kincaid again. But of course she had not wanted to see him like this!

Her dark brows knitted together as she searched his face. Perhaps he had asked for the minister because he thought he was dying.

Impulsively, she grasped his wrist and searched for his pulse. The throbbing against her thumb was faint, but steady.

She heard the sound of the departing wagon wheels crunching through the snow. In a moment the door opened and her father hurried back inside, latching the door against the bitter night.

"What do you think?" He rushed to her side, rubbing his hands for warmth.

"His pulse is weak," she whispered. "Father, did the bartender tell you anything else? About who shot him, I mean?"

He hesitated, then spoke quietly. "When the men awoke me, they said he had been robbed and shot."

For a moment Jenny was speechless. Then she jumped to her feet, her dark eyes blazing.

"That Benson! I'll bet he did it. I disliked him from the moment I saw him."

"Jenny, we mustn't jump to conclusions." Her father leaned over Clint's feet to stoke up the fire. "In the morning, we'll borrow a cot for him."

Her mind struggled to grasp this strange turn of events, but all she could think was that Clint Kincaid was here—in her house. Here, where she could sit by his side, pray for him, care for him.

She turned back to her father, her anger melting at the sight of his weary face. "You've had so little rest. Go get some sleep." She touched his arm. "I'll watch awhile . . . ."

He hesitated, glancing back at the young man on the pallet, but then agreed. "Maybe I'll just close my eyes for a spell. But call me if there's any change."

"Yes, I will," Jenny assured him. After he stretched out on the sofa, she drew a chair closer to the fire and got as warm and comfortable as possible. Then she stared down at Clint Kincaid. *Lord, please let him live.*

The March wind howled around the cabin, a low moan that carried with it an almost ominous threat. Still shivering, she closed her eyes and prayed for him, this man she scarcely knew. Whether he was a man of God, she was uncertain. But God who in his infinite mercy loved all creatures great and small, loved Clint Kincaid as well.

She opened her eyes, and stared down at the thick blond hair; it looked like spun gold in the firelight. Was there a woman in his life, she wondered anxiously, a woman waiting for him—somewhere. Unaccountably, that possibility saddened her.

Throughout the dark night, Jenny sat by his side, testing his forehead for fever, checking his weak pulse, feeding the fire to warm him.

As the darkness gave way to a cold gray dawn, Jenny slipped into the kitchen to make coffee, her bones aching and stiff.

Hearing her movements, her father stirred on the sofa.

"Any change?" he called softly.

"None," she sighed, wearily lifting the coffee pot.

"Jenny," her father rose, fully awake, "go and lie down now. I'll take over."

She glanced at her father. His face was rested, his eyes bright with the promise of a better day.

"All right," she agreed, turning toward her bedroom. When she crawled under the quilts, the soft comfort of her bed brought a moan of relief. But when she closed her eyes, Clint's inert body filled her thoughts.

Her lips moved in prayer, a prayer that was never finished as exhaustion overtook her.

Jenny awoke to her father's tread across the floor. She blinked sleepily, wondering what time it was. Then her thoughts flew to Clint Kincaid and she bolted out of bed, smoothing the wrinkled clothing she'd been too tired to change. She opened the door and stepped into the living room, fighting back a rush of uneasiness.

Clint was lying in the same position, stretched before the fire; yet he was changed, drastically changed! Jenny blinked sleepy eyes, then gasped in surprise. The beard was gone, and the clean, masculine profile was even more appealing than before.

"I thought he needed a good shave," her father smiled. "We must be able to see his colorings. But with all that thick beard, there was scarcely any skin visible."

He lay before her like a Greek god, the perfectly chiseled features softened in sleep. She had already memorized the gold-tipped lashes and straight nose during her vigil. Now her gaze ran over the lean jawline and square chin. A determined chin she thought—perhaps he may even be stubborn if he took a notion.

"His pulse is stronger," her father was saying. "Here, have some coffee, daughter." A warm mug was placed in her hand. "Once or twice he stirred, but then he went right off to sleep. "I think he's going to be all right,—the good Lord willing."

Jenny smiled up at her father. His tone was confident and dispelled her fearful mood.

"Then I'll fix breakfast," she said, her practical nature asserting itself now that the crisis had passed.

"No need. I've already made gruel," he motioned her toward the chair by the fire. "Just sit and drink your coffee. You've had a wearying night."

"All right," she gave him a weak smile as she settled into the chair.

As she sipped the strong coffee, her eyes rested on Clint. Again, her heart began to pound erratically, and she realized that she had never tired of looking at him.

"The doctor has come," her father said, striding to the door.

The cold air rushed in through the open door, and Jenny's gaze lifted eagerly to the vast blue sky, cloudless for the first time in days. Maybe the worst of winter had ended at last.

"Good morning, Frank," her father took the doctor's coat. "Glad you could stop by. Doctorin' isn't my calling."

The doctor, spare and tall, nodded briskly. "I wouldn't have thought a man could lose that much blood and survive the night. Good thing he's strong and healthy."

Since Jenny wasn't needed for the moment, she took the opportunity to slip to the kitchen and pour warm water from the kettle into a small pan. Lifting a clean washcloth from the shelf, she returned to her room and pulled a fresh cake of soap from her dresser drawer.

The splash of warm water on her face brought a pleasant tingle, and she reveled in the sweet-smelling soap on her skin. It would be too bad when her supply ran out. She certainly couldn't wash her face in the strong lye soap folks around here used on their clothes.

She pulled a fresh cotton dress over her head, listening intently to the murmur of voices from the next room. Another voice had been added—a weak voice, yet its deep timber was unmistakable. Clint!

Hurriedly, she buttoned the lace collar of her dress, then peered into her small hand mirror. The lantern from the table cast flickering images over her smooth face, pale against the starry depths of her eyes. Placing the mirror back on the table, she patted down her hair and opened the door.

Her father and the doctor were kneeling beside Clint. His eyes were open, but his face was twisted with pain.

"You'll just have to take it easy now, young man." The doctor spoke with authority. "The Reverend has

30

offered you a place to stay till you're stronger. I think that's a fine idea. And you couldn't find a better nurse than Jenny here."

Suddenly all eyes were on her as she paused in the doorway, but she saw only the intense gaze that softened perceptibly as Clint's eyes found hers.

Instinctively, she hurried across to stand before him, her shyness melting.

"Welcome back," she smiled down at him.

"Yep, you had a close call," the doctor was saying. "Mighty lucky for you the bartender heard a shot and decided to investigate."

At the doctor's words, a cold light flickered in Clint's eyes. "Yeah, lucky." The full lips tightened into a thin line. "How long before I can get up?"

"Depends on how fast you heal," the doctor replied. "I'll be back to check on you. In the meantime, stay put. You have some mighty nice folks to look after you."

Clint turned to stare into the fire, slipping into a quiet somber mood.

"Would you like some breakfast?" Jenny asked.

"I'm not hungry," he sighed. "Maybe just some coffee, if you don't mind."

"I don't mind at all," she answered, hurrying to the kitchen, grateful that she could take some action. Glancing toward the closed front door, she caught the low hum of voices outside. No doubt, her father and the doctor were discussing Clint's condition.

As she poured the coffee, then lifted the steaming mug, a sense of uneasiness crept over her. She could understand Clint's anger and bitterness, yet she had no idea what to say to console him. Forcing her mind back to the task, she returned to the fire, the mug extended.

"Here you are," she smiled, carefully placing the mug in his hand.

Her heart quickened as his fingers brushed her's. She felt his disconcerting glance again, and she quickly averted her eyes, hoping that her face did not reveal the strange fascination that filled her each time she looked at Clint Kincaid.

"I can't tell you how sorry I am, inconveniencing you and your father this way," Clint was saying. "I remember asking for your father, but I only wanted his prayers." He stared down into the coffee, a reflective expression on his lean face. "I'll be moving along in a day or so."

"There's no hurry," she said quickly. "You must give yourself time to recover your strength. And as for prayers, I—we haven't stopped praying all night."

He sipped his coffee, contemplating her words. "Then I must thank you again. It had to be your prayers that saved me."

"Mr. Kincaid—"

"Clint," he interrupted. "Please call me Clint. I'd consider it a favor. After all, you and your father helped save my life."

"The doctor deserves the credit—and God." she corrected with a smile. "Clint," she tested the name softly, "who shot you?"

The blue eyes leapt to hers, the square jaw clenching momentarily. "Benson."

"I knew it!" she cried. "That dreadful man!"

Clint released a pent-up sigh. "I had money on me. There's only one thing a man like that has on his mind—and that's money. Unless, of course, it's women . . . uh, forgive me, Jenny."

32

She shook her dark head, ignoring his last words. "What will you do now?"

He turned to stare at the fire, a bleak expression crossing his face. "I don't know."

She scooted to the edge of the chair, wanting desperately to offer Clint hope. "Perhaps we can help. There are members of our congregation who—"

"No!" he cut in, his voice gruff. "I'll manage. I don't take charity."

The bitterness in his tone disturbed her. She frowned, searching her mind for words to comfort him, while some deeper instinct silenced them before they were spoken. He was hurt, angry, bitter. This was not the time to speak, but rather to listen. She sat rigid, waiting for him to speak.

"I should never have gone to that saloon with Benson," he finally muttered, more to himself, it seemed, than to her. "Being here in your home, enjoying your hospitality and pleasuring in the company of good people—that should have been enough. But Benson's suggestion to go to the Lucky Dollar seemed like a good idea at the time. I knew once I went back up to the mine, I wouldn't be returning to town for days."

He paused, his hand lightly touching the bandage that covered his upper chest and right shoulder, as though he suddenly remembered the impact of the bullet. "After we had a few drinks," he paused, frowning, "we left the saloon by the back door. He had wanted to hitch the horses to the rail out back."

The mouth tightened as he spoke and a flush of anger crept over his face. "I was walking a few steps ahead of him; then suddenly, I felt him breathing down my neck. I turned around to see the barrel of his

33

gun. We struggled, then . . . he shot me as I fell. Luckily, he was a poor marksman."

Jenny's heart was hammering in her chest as she sat listening to his story. She could appreciate how difficult it must be to talk about it.

"I still think you are very fortunate," she said, touching his arm reassuringly.

A draft of cold air filled the room as the front door opened, and her father entered.

Jenny jerked her hand back and folded her fingers tightly in her lap. Her father was shivering in his thin flannel shirt, a worried frown on his face. *Poor father!* she thought miserably. There never seemed to be any rest for him.

He hurried across to the fire, his fingers extended to absorb some warmth. "The doctor is stopping by the Sheriff's office, Clint. We thought you would want to give a description of the man who shot you."

"It was Benson," Jenny replied, her tone registering her scorn for the man.

Her father nodded. "I suspected that. Then surely we can stop him before—"

"I doubt it," Clint interjected. "He's miles from here by now. His mining claim is worthless. I realize now that he was only hanging around Cripple Creek until he could steal enough money to get out. You folks provided him with a good hot meal, and I furnished the money."

Joseph heard the bitter tale, spoken from between clenched teeth, then turned back to the fire. "We can't be certain he's left the territory," he said after a thoughtful pause. "And you must press charges against him, to prevent his repeating the crime with some other innocent victim."

"I should have known better," Clint sighed. "Although he worked the claim next to mine, I sensed the kind of man he was. I should never have ridden into town with him."

"Don't blame yourself," Jenny burst out in defense. An awkward silence followed, bringing a blush to her cheeks. She glanced at her father and met a look of surprise. Beneath knitted brows he was studying her carefully now, and in response, she averted her gaze to her hands, clasping her fingers tighter.

How emotional she must sound to her father. And of course to Clint! She was becoming too involved, she knew that now. Her father had often warned her of the dangers of losing objectivity in their ministry. She swallowed, forcing herself to keep quiet before she made a fool of herself again.

"Well, we have a change in weather, at last," her father pointed toward the window, where a blazing sun had driven away the remainder of the storm clouds. "Bill says the snow is melting everywhere, and that merchants are shoveling the slush from the sidewalks in Cripple Creek. Let's pray the winter is over."

The encouraging note in her father's voice drew Jenny's attention. "I do need to buy some groceries," she smiled at him. "Since the weather is improved, perhaps I'll walk down to the store."

"Some fresh air would do you good," her father agreed. "I told Joe Warren I would deliver his orders up to Bull Hill and Spring Creek. In return, he has insisted that we fill our own larder, as well."

Jenny stared at her father. Free groceries? When her father had mentioned this errand at the dinner table the night before, the possibility of his work being rewarded with groceries had escaped her! A bright smile tilted her full lips, and her eyes sparkled hopefully.

Why had she allowed doubt and fear to overrule common sense? Her father had always provided for them, despite a few anxious moments. She must exercise more faith and less pessimism; otherwise, she might start to sound like her friend Maude!

"Well, that's very nice of Mr. Warren." she said, suppressing a laugh and reaching for her bonnet. From the corner of her eye, she was aware of Clint Kincaid watching her curiously. "I do hope you'll feel better." She forced a pleasant yet noncommittal tone to her voice. From now on, she was determined to keep a tighter reign on her emotions. After all, she knew virtually nothing about the man, and she certainly didn't approve of the company he kept.

But the heartstopping grin he gave her sent her mind reeling in confusion, and she hurried out the door before her expression gave her away.

Jenny was still trying to push Clint to the back of her mind when she turned down Bennett Avenue, basking in the sunshine that was almost blinding after the lifeless gray days. From some of the rooftops, shopkeepers were shoveling away the lingering clumps of snow. The roofs, like the flimsy, green-lumber buildings, could endure little strain and often collapsed beneath the weight of winter's blizzards.

But today brought the promise of spring, and Jenny lifted her face to the golden sunshine, delighting in the penetrating warmth. That warmth seemed to draw from her very soul the long cold mood of winter.

Others were taking advantage of the pleasant weather, Jenny noted, glancing at the carts, carriages, and wagons that lined the streets. Donkey's brayed beneath loads of mining supplies, and farther down, a rancher's sleigh was being loaded with large bales of hay to feed the stock deprived of meadow grass during the blizzard.

Jenny's curious gaze returned to the sidewalk, where a group of lean and hungry-looking miners were striding into saloons. Strange how the saloons had become the social centers, Jenny thought. Cripple Creek had been erected in great haste, with little planning as to the order of things. The saloons outnumbered the other establishments two to one and were sandwiched in among other businesses. Consequently, every other door seemed to lead to a saloon.

Just ahead the batwing door of the Lucky Dollar swung open, and instinctively Jenny's booted steps quickened. She tried to keep her eyes on the path before her, but the memory of Clint's presence here ignited her curiosity. There was no way she could resist a quick peek into the dim interior.

She slowed her pace as she passed the door and had a fleeting glimpse of a waxed mahogany bar where a knot of men were huddled. Her gaze rested on the man nearest the door who was slumped over the bar, his felt hat slung low on his forehead. Then, as though sensing eyes on him, he turned to stare at her, lifting a whiskey bottle in mock salute.

The door swung shut, and she hurried on, her mind branded with the memory of that dim, smoke-filled room. How could Clint enjoy a place like that? And did he make a habit of frequenting the saloons?

She hurried under the striped awning of Warren and

Williams grocery, her gloved hand pressing the latch of the heavy wooden door.

Upon entering, a rush of warmth from the pot-bellied stove in the center of the room brought a glow to her cheeks. Her dark lashes opened wider in an effort to adjust her vision from the glaring sunlight to the dim interior. Sectioned shelves of tinned goods, five-cent cigars, confectionary and bulk items reached from the oiled, wooden floors to the high, drafty ceilings. Jenny paused, studying the variety of items.

"Good morning, Miss Townley," Joe Warren called to her. "It's good to see you again."

"Good morning, Mr. Warren," Jenny smiled at the heavyset, gray-haired man whose starched white apron dignified the cluttered grocery.

Methodically, she began to gather up the items she needed, too occupied with her task to notice a pair of piercing, gray eyes.

"Miss Townley!"

Jenny turned to face Myrtle Tubbs, an older member of the congregation, whose sharp tongue had earned her the reputation of being the town gossip. The beak face and hawkish eyes probed Jenny with unbridled curiosity.

"Is it true?" she demanded in her shrill voice.

Jenny blinked. "I beg your pardon?"

"Has Reverend Townley taken in that man who was drunk and brawling at the saloon? Even got himself shot, I hear tell." Her wiry brows were twin peaks of disapproval.

Jenny struggled to frame a reply that would not add grist to her gossip mill.

"They brought a man to us who had no place to go," Jenny answered carefully, "who, in fact, was

38

neither drunken nor brawling, but rather a victim of circumstance."

"A circumstance he brought on himself, I vow!" Myrtle continued. "Never should've been in the saloon in the first place. Of course," she leaned closer, "I understand that many of our leading citizens frequent the Lucky Dollar."

"Mrs. Tubbs," Jenny forced a smile, "my father insisted that I hurry back, so I must ask you to excuse me." She bowed politely and turned away.

No doubt Myrtle Tubbs would criticize her for being rude, but that was preferable to saying anything that would add to her arsenal of rumors and lies.

Hurriedly, Jenny grabbed the remainder of her groceries, careful to avoid Myrtle's accusing smirk. She placed her supplies along the counter and waited for Joe Warren to tally up.

"If you want to know anything, just ask Myrtle!" he teased under his breath. "But this time she may be right."

"About what?"

"About the stranger who's staying at your place. I hear the money that was stolen from him came straight from the gambling tables. He *is* a big–time gambler, you know." He tilted his gray head to study her curiously. "Or maybe you didn't know."

CHAPTER 3

FIRELIGHT FLICKERED OVER THE WALLS of the cabin as Jenny curled up in the chair, reading from her book of poems. She had been staring at the same line for the past five minutes, while her thoughts wandered to the man slumped on the sofa.

The only sounds in the room were the snapping of the flames in the fireplace and the scratching of Joseph's pen on his tablet as he sat at the kitchen table, scribbling his sermon. Occasionally he glanced up from his work, his gaze drifting from Jenny to Clint Kincaid, the frown deepening on his furrowed brow.

Had he noticed her quiet mood? She had been unable to enter into the supper conversation, although Clint was profuse in his compliments of her meal. The grocery store gossip gnawed at her peace of mind until her mental efforts to defend him had left her emotionally drained.

Was it true? she wondered. Was Clint what they had claimed—a brawler, a gambler?

She swallowed hard, unable to imagine this gentle, soft-spoken man in any of those roles. Slowly she lowered the book from her line of vision, and her eyes crept across the room to the sofa where Clint lay.

His fresh clothes were a welcome sight. The bartender had brought Clint's saddlebag that, fortunately, contained a change of clothing. The rest of his possessions, she supposed, were at his mining camp.

He was staring into the fire, lost in his own thoughts. She welcomed this opportunity to study him in repose, hoping in these unguarded moments to pick up some clue as to his true nature.

Assessing his character was difficult. What she saw when she looked at him was a startlingly handsome man. With the thick, golden beard removed, the lean cheeks, sharply defined jaw and chin brought the face into proportion. The firelight softened his bright gold hair to a gleaming tawny color. And while the hair, still unruly, tumbled over his brow and carelessly brushed his collar, it seemed to add a dash of mystery and adventure to his sun-glazed face. Thick brown brows arched sharply above the blue eyes that lightened or deepened with his moods. It was impossible for her to analyze this strange man.

He turned suddenly, his speculative look capturing hers. Her cheeks burned with the knowledge that he had caught her staring wide-eyed—again.

"Would you mind reading aloud?" His gaze dropped to the book in her hands. "Robert Browning is one of my favorite poets."

Blankly, she followed his eyes to the book whose pages fluttered beneath trembling fingers. She would feel ridiculous reading poetry to Clint Kincaid, and yet, how could she refuse?

"Do you mind?" he asked gently.

"I . . . of course not," she stammered glancing at her father.

His pen was poised over the lined paper, while his gaze remained fixed on the notes before him.

Jenny gripped the book, moistened her lips, and cleared her throat, mentally rehearsing the first line. A twig snapped in the fire as Clint waited.

Finally, summoning her courage, she started to read:

"She should never have looked at me if she meant I should not love her . . ." she began shyly. As the lovely verses drifted into the soft silence of the cabin, she felt Clint's eyes intent on her.

She clutched the book tighter, trying desperately to center her concentration on the poem. Her voice, small and shy at first, gained strength with each word. Caught up in the beauty of "Christina," she soon forgot her self-consciousness and became absorbed in the nostalgic mood. Jenny's voice reached a crescendo on the final verse, then died away as a reverent silence, like an eulogy, drifted over the room.

"I *knew* you should be in a school back East!" her father exclaimed, suddenly shattering the sensitive mood. "You would make a fine teacher in some university."

"Father, you gave me a choice before we left St. Louis, remember? I chose to come here."

Joseph Townley sighed, his bony hand thrusting the pad aside with an air of impatience. "Well, you deserve better," he mumbled.

"I can understand why you say that, sir," Clint spoke up. "Not only does she have a sharp mind, she's a rare combination of beauty and sweetness."

Clint looked at her thoughtfully. "I must agree with him, Jenny. You do seem out of place in this rough western town."

She looked from one man to the other. How could they be so certain about where she should be or what she should be doing? Furthermore, it was embarrassing to be assessed so openly, as though she hadn't a mind of her own.

"I'm old enough to make my own decisions," she countered, her tone firm. Then with a sudden burst, she exclaimed, "Father, I don't want to be anywhere else. And I don't wish to discuss this ever again!"

An uncharacteristic display of temper registered briefly on Joseph's face. "You're right, of course. You are old enough to make your own decisions. And I won't question your good judgment again." He looked across at Clint. "Jennifer is very loyal. I don't know how I could ever manage without her."

With that admission he pushed back his chair. "I need some exercise." He rose and stretched his arms over his head. "Jenny, if you'll fetch the flour we owe Mrs. Jacobs, I'll take a quick stroll over to their cabin before bedtime."

Wordlessly, Jenny scrambled to her feet and hurried to the kitchen. She had completely forgotten the flour she had borrowed from Maude, but of course she hadn't been herself lately.

She lifted the tin cup from the open shelf that served as her cupboard, then reached for her new sack of flour. As she dipped the flour, her mind darted back to the conversation with Myrtle Tubbs, and worse, with Mr. Warren.

Sifting the flour into Maude's tin cup, Jenny thought about the vile accusations made against Clint. There would be no peace for her until she confronted him about the matter. Perhaps it was none of her affair, but she determined that while her father was out of the house she would speak with Clint about the rumors.

"Tell Maude hello for me," she said, handing her father the cup of flour.

"Yes, I will," he smiled, pulling on his tweed coat, threadbare at the elbows.

Jenny followed him to the door and lifted the latch, and hugged her arms to herself as the cold air greeted them.

"Be careful," she called into the darkness. "The path is still icy in spots."

She closed the door on his retreating figure then turned to face Clint, her mind busily searching for the right way to approach him.

"You're very protective of him, aren't you?" Clint asked.

"Yes, I suppose I am," she replied, crossing to the fireplace to warm herself. "You see, my mother died when I was born, so we have only each other."

"What about your family?" she asked curiously. "You've never told us anything about yourself."

"Not a lot to tell," he replied. The tone was intended to be casual, but Jenny had not missed the subtle tightening of his mouth as he spoke. "I'm just a drifter, like a lot of other guys wandering around Cripple Creek."

Jenny clasped her hands behind her, lacing her fingers together to still their fidgeting. She could feel the warmth of the fire searing her arms through the cotton sleeves, yet she felt cold to the bone. She *had* to pursue this conversation, even though she wasn't sure she wanted to know the answer.

No, you aren't just another drifter, Clint Kincaid, she thought. *And you aren't like the other men wandering around out there.*

"Who are you . . . really?" she asked. "Where do you come from?"

She was aware that Clint probably considered her rudely inquisitive, but she and her father had very likely saved his life. They had a right to know something about this man they had prayed for during the past tense hours.

He leaned back against the pillow, his bronze face, inscrutable.

"Why are you so interested?"

"Because I heard a rumor today . . . "

"Go on," he prompted, regarding her with indifference. "It can't be that bad. Or," he hesitated, "can it?"

A worried frown rumpled her smooth brow. The words were slow in coming. As gently as possible, she related the ugly rumors and then waited, breath bated, for his response.

A sardonic grin tilted the corners of his mouth, and a cold light flared in the depths of his eyes.

"What do *you* think, Jenny? Do you believe what you heard?"

"No, I don't! No matter what they say, or what you *don't* say, I believe you are a good person," she answered. "I just don't understand why you choose to be so mysterious, that's all."

He chuckled softly and stared into the dancing fire. "I'm not a good person, Jenny," he said dully, "not by your standards. I do frequent saloons, and I have been known to brawl. But I did not fight Benson or anyone else that night. I like to play blackjack," he

45

grinned, obviously aware that he was incriminating himself, "but I had not been gambling either."

"And the money?" she blurted.

Clearly, she was overstepping the boundary of polite interest. Still, she could not seem to stop herself. Her cheeks tingled beneath his shrewd sweeping glance.

"The money was mine," he repeated.

A moment later the hard glare in his eyes softened as though he were suddenly amused by a private joke.

"I just remembered the reason I never married." The lopsided grin tilted his mouth again. "I cannot tolerate giving an account of myself to anyone."

"I—I'm sorry," she stammered, dropping into the chair and staring blankly at her book. "I had no right to question you about your personal affairs."

"You had every right. After all, you and your father have taken me in, obviously to the chagrin of most of the townspeople. I just don't wish to elaborate on my family or my past at the moment."

"Please, Clint, do reconsider," Jenny pressed. "Surely your family would want to know about your injury?"

The brows lifted. "Yes, and they would immediately dispatch a carriage to fetch me back to Denver. And when I recovered I would find myself again firmly implanted in the family business. No thanks."

Denver? The family business?

The words brought a pleasant sense of relief despite the bitterness with which they were spoken. Jenny's instincts were right! This was no common drifter, as he would have her believe. He was a member of a prominent Denver family, no doubt, who had simply struck out on his own to try his luck at mining. Surely that was not so different from many other adventurous young men who had rushed to Denver in the late fifties, or even to California when the cry of gold at Sutter's Mill had inflamed the nation.

"So I was right about you, after all," she smiled.

"Now hold on!" he laughed. "Just because you don't think I'm the usual sort of drifter does not change other things—like the color of my soul, which is rather black at the moment."

"But Clint," a smile lit her face, "you can come to church with us and—"

"No, Jenny! Let the town gossips say what they will. I won't become one of your devout church members. I'm sorry. You and your father have been very good to me, but I cannot pretend to be something I'm not."

She should have expected that answer from him. Besides, as a minister's daughter, she knew well that one can never save a soul by shoving him into a church pew or shouting about hell and damnation. No, if one couldn't serve as a living example of faith, then no amount of preaching would make any difference.

She lifted her head and offered him a smile. "I'll never expect you to be someone you're not, Clint Kincaid. So there! As for your parents, don't you think they would want to help you if they knew your situation?"

"Yes, they would. But I can't take their money any more, not after declaring my independence so firmly. I was determined not to twiddle my life away behind a desk at the lumber mill. I wanted to make my own fortune, and I shall! I'll just have to come up with some more money, that's all."

Lumber mill! The last pieces of the puzzle were falling into place. "How are you going to get by in the meantime?" she asked softly. "It will take weeks to regain your strength."

"I'm strong," he muttered. "It won't take long for me to be active again. As for money, I will have to find work where I can. I've never shunned hard work."

"But Clint," she shook her head. "there are hundreds of miners roaming the territory, looking for work. Since the silver mine closed, the mining population here has doubled, perhaps tripled. And all the people who can't get jobs in the gold mines are grabbing all the other available jobs. Many are still unemployed. I know this is true," she added gently, "because some have come to us for help."

"And now I'm just one more busted miner imposing on you," he concluded harshly. "Eating your food, taking up space—"

"Don't say that," she scolded. "I only mention this because I feel you should not endanger your health further by taking a job that would require hard labor. From what I hear, that's the only kind of work available."

"I'll manage. Just don't concern—" He broke off suddenly, his teeth clenched in pain.

"What is it?" Jenny rushed to his side, watching the color drain from his face.

"I twisted the wrong way," he moaned softly, the gold-tipped lashes fluttering over hazy blue eyes. He relaxed a little and looked at her intently, the pained expression slipping from his face as she leaned over him to adjust his pillow.

She straightened the blankets around him and was about to leave, when his left hand gripped her arm.

"What . . .?" she began to speak, then forgot what she was going to say as she was drawn into the blazing depths of his eyes. She was not conscious of lowering her head, just as she was not conscious of Clint pulling her closer. But when their lips met in a sweet and tender kiss, the effect was more electrifying than any emotion she had ever experienced.

Her senses reeled, and when her lids fluttered open, she was staring into liquid blue.

She straightened slightly, then froze as softly he repeated one of the verses she had read to him:

"She should never have looked at me if she meant I should not love her . . ."

A tremulous smile curved Jenny's lips, then slowly faded as Clint suddenly released her and turned his face to the wall.

"I shouldn't have done that," he said huskily. "I'm sorry."

Jenny's mind whirled with emotions. What did he mean? Did he wish he hadn't kissed her?

At her silence, he turned his head to stare at her, and there was an expression of pain—a different kind of pain—twisting his chiseled lips.

"I'll be leaving tomorrow," he said in a clear, firm tone. "I cannot impose on you and your father any longer."

"You're too weak to leave," she argued.

"You're wrong, Jenny," a smile tilted his mouth. "I am much too weak to stay."

Jenny felt her face redden.

How many boyfriends have you had?" he asked, amusement flickering in his eyes.

"Why, I . . . there has never been time for romance. One beau in St. Louis, but . . . " her voice

49

trailed away, as she found herself embarassed to explain to this worldly man that she had never loved anyone.

"With the exception of this beau in St. Louis, I suspect one reason there has been no time for romance is because no man has ever been good enough for you."

"That's a cruel thing for you to say. Cruel and unfair!" she snapped.

"I mean that as a compliment, Jenny," his voice, like his smile, was sadly wistful. "You are a very special lady. You must never let your heart maneuver you into a relationship unworthy of you."

His words soothed her rising temper, and she bit her lip, struggling to regain a composure that seemed to vanish every time she was near Clint. She took a deep breath. How was she ever going to set a good example for him when her temper kept getting in the way?

"It's amusing to me," she responded lightly, "how you and Father are so adept at deciding my destiny. Apparently, you think I'm quite empty-headed, or a puppet on a string. But, no, Mr. Kincaid! Despite your rather prudish impression of me, I assure you that I make my own decisions. And that includes my choice of friends."

"Friends?" he laughed softly. "Truthfully, you intrigue me. You are such an interesting combination of sweetness and honesty and . . . spirit. And I am quite certain that when you choose a man, he will be the right one for you. In the meantime," he shifted his gaze to the small window, "don't waste any more of your time on me."

Jenny slumped into her chair. She could not

possibly think straight in the presence of Clint Kincaid!

He spoke once more, breaking the silence.

"I'll be leaving, Jenny. Tomorrow."

She had no doubt that he would do just that.

CHAPTER 4

JENNY PUSHED THROUGH THE CROWD along Bennett Avenue, taking large gulps of the clean mountain air to steady her nerves. Her pale face was drawn, but resolute.

She had just completed the most reckless mission of her life, and no doubt she would pay dearly for her actions. But she could not disobey the leadings of her heart.

She turned the corner, leaving the noise of Cripple Creek behind as she faced the steep hill leading up to the cluster of cabins. Clint might already be gone by now. She stretched her long legs into quicker steps. He had adamantly refused to stay on, despite her protests, despite her father's gentle insistence.

And now . . . he would find out what she had done, how she had gone to the bank to use their telephone for a call to Denver. She took a wild chance that the family's lumber business was listed as Kincaid Lumber Mill and could scarcely believe her ears when she discovered she had guessed correctly. In a few moments Clint's father had spoken into the phone, and she had told him everything. The soft-spoken man voiced his appreciation for her call and assured her that he would be on the next train to Cripple Creek.

Jenny swallowed against the dry ache in her throat and struggled to draw more oxygen into her lungs. Clint would be furious with her! The knowledge left her weak. But what did she have to lose? It was obvious he did not intend to see her again. And he had refused to consider attending their church services. What hope did she have in a relationship with this strong-willed man?

Weary, she untied the strings of her bonnet to bare her head to the gentle breeze. At least Mr. Kincaid would see to his son's medical needs, perhaps even take him home to Denver, as Clint had feared. But maybe Denver was where he belonged, she consoled herself; he obviously had not fared well in Cripple Creek.

Her breath was coming in short gasps by the time she turned up the cleared path to her front door. Her eyes watered and her throat ached. And something deep inside ached even more. She had never before cared for a man, and the knowledge that she was now gripped with some emotion that was foreign to her merely added to her frustration.

As she entered the yard, the cabin door opened, and Clint walked out. He seemed to have shrunk in the past couple of days, but she suspected it was because he was stooping slightly to protect his chest and upper arm from the pull of the tight bandages.

"Well, thank you again, sir," he said, and Jenny noted the weakness in his voice.

He had no business being out in this cold! She longed to throw her arms around him to restrain him from going. But, of course, she could not do that.

Then she thought of his father, who might be boarding a train this very minute. Help was on the way, she sighed, as he turned to bid her goodbye.

"Clint, will you be stopping by for a visit sometime?" she asked. "Or . . . are you leaving Cripple Creek?"

"I'm not sure of my plans yet," he shrugged.

"Clint, won't you accept a small love offering from the church?" Joseph touched his shoulder.

"No, sir," Clint shook his head resolutely. "I couldn't do that. As I mentioned earlier, I have a friend at one of the hotels. I can stay there temporarily."

Jenny stepped aside, her heart wrenching as she watched him pick his way unsteadily down the path.

"Don't forget," her father called after him, "your horse is at Welty's Stable."

"Yes, I'll go there first," he called over his shoulder. "And thanks for everything." He turned back, his glance resting on Jenny for a mere second. Then he turned and walked away.

Jenny stared after the tall, lean figure in the patched buckskin jacket for a long moment. Then, sick at heart, she opened the door and entered the cabin. Her knees were trembling after her brisk walk to town, and the strain of the past day seemed to crash in upon her.

Her hand felt like dead weight as she lifted her fingers to unbutton her cloak. The film of perspiration that had formed on her face during her frantic walk now dripped down her neck, dampening the collar of her gray broadcloth dress.

"You must not fret yourself," her father said, upon entering the cabin. "We've done the best we could do for him. The rest is up to God."

"I'm not certain Clint Kincaid even believes in God!" Jenny responded.

"But we do," her father reminded her. "And we will be praying for him."

"Oh, father!" Jenny burst into tears. "I've just done something very . . . daring. I only hope I haven't made a terrible mistake."

"What on earth are you talking about?"

"I went to the bank and telephoned Clint's father in Denver. He will be arriving on the next train."

Joseph stared at her, unblinking, then he sank into a chair. "How did you know where to contact his father?" he finally asked.

"I pieced together what Clint told me about his family. I believed it was the best thing."

Joseph shook his head as a tiny smile hovered at the corners of his mouth. "You may be right, but I don't know how our headstrong young friend will react to the unexpected arrival of his father!"

"Like dynamite going off at the mines!" Jenny cried. "He will never speak to me again, Father. I'm certain of that. You see, he is very proud," she sniffed, trying to check her flow of tears, "and quite determined to manage on his own. But how can he? He's flat broke with no job and he's ill."

"Try not to worry," her father patted her arm. "The deed is done. We have to turn the situation over to God and trust Him to work things out."

"Yes, I know that," Jenny sighed.

But had she already taken too much into her own hands? She had done what she felt was best for Clint.

Like a mother, watching a child carelessly toddle toward an open fire, she had reacted instinctively. Yet now she knew she had wantonly violated Clint's privacy. She had no right —no right at all!

Jenny took a deep breath and forced herself to consider her father's advice. It *was* done. She must turn the matter over to God.

The next evening, Jenny moved listlessly about the kitchen, trying to force some enthusiasm into her baking, when a brisk tapping sounded at her front door.

Had Clint returned, after all?

She grabbed a checkerboard cuptowel and dried her hands, then rushed for the door. If Clint had come, what would she say to him? She frantically patted her hair into the smooth knot at the nape of her neck.

When she opened the door, a distinguished gentleman dressed in dark woolen coat and trousers stood on the slab step. At the sight of her, he removed his fashionable hat, revealing neatly-styled silver hair. The eyes that flickered over her were a shade deeper than Clint's and with the realization of his identity, her breath caught in her throat.

"Good evening," he nodded. "Is this Reverend Townley's residence?"

"Yes, it is,' Jenny replied, keeping her voice steady. "Did you want to see my father?"

"That depends." A smile softened the thin mouth. "I am Calvin Kincaid, Clint's father."

"How do you do?" Jenny smiled. "I'm Jennifer Townley. Won't you please come in?"

As she stepped aside, the man entered their modest cabin and Jenny felt suddenly nervous and self-conscious. Wealth and status seemed to emanate from him, from the proud set of his silver head to the cut of his well-tailored gray suit.

"Would you like to sit down?" she asked belatedly. "I'm afraid my father is not at home, but perhaps I could help you."

"Thank you," he replied, seating himself on the edge of the sofa.

She was thankful again for the few good pieces of furniture they had wrestled onto the wagon when they moved west. At least this man could see that she and her father recognized quality, even though their tiny cramped cabin left much to be desired.

"Miss Townley, I have been unable to locate Clint," he said, glancing across at her with deeply troubled eyes.

He was obviously a man who wasted no time in useless conversation. Jenny was grateful for that. Trying to ignore the obvious issue, for even a few minutes, would have made the meeting even more difficult.

"Did you inquire at all the hotels?" she asked, her pulse quickening with alarm.

"Yes, I did," he sighed, balancing his black top-hat on the perfectly-creased knee of his trousers. "I hoped perhaps he might have returned here." The sharp blue eyes scanned the interior of the cabin. "But I see that he has not."

"No," she sighed. "Mr. Kincaid, I haven't seen Clint since yesterday morning when I called you. I do know that his horse was boarded at Welty's Stable. You might inquire there. If the horse is gone, perhaps he rode up to check on his mining claim. But he was in no condition to ride!"

"Why do you say that?" he leaned closer.

"He was still running a fever when he left. And I assume the loss of blood has left him weak and dizzy." She paused, realizing her answer would only serve to further distress his father. "But, as you know, he is very determined." She tried to lighten her tone as she forced a cheerful smile. "Perhaps his strong will can carry him through."

"Yes, it usually does," he mumbled, the silver brows knitted in contemplation. His blue eyes were every bit as penetrating as Clint's, but there the resemblance ended. The older man's features were sharply drawn, and his skin was pale compared to his son's golden hue.

"Miss Townley, could you tell me exactly what happened to Clint?" An urgency crept into his smooth voice. "He was robbed, you said? Have they caught the man who did it?"

Jennifer shifted uncomfortably, her eyes straying from his worried face.

"Perhaps you should ask the Sheriff," she replied. "I really cannot say." She had already betrayed Clint by calling his father. She would not add insult to injury. Calvin Kincaid would have to learn the details on his own.

Sensing her reserve, he came quickly to his feet.

"Yes, I shall do that. In fact, I'll ask the Sheriff to help me locate Clint. But first, I'll check Welty's Stable as you have suggested." He hesitated, twirling the brim of his hat with quick nervous fingers.

"Miss Townley, I want to thank you for all you've done," Calvin Kincaid bowed politely. "In fact, I would like very much to repay you for your trouble." He reached inside his coat pocket to extract a slim leather wallet.

"Oh, no!" Jenny protested. "I couldn't possibly accept anything for helping Clint." My father would be offended if I did. Helping those in need is a part of our mission to Cripple Creek."

"Then could I make a contribution to your church?" he asked.

"Thank you, but we don't have a church building yet. We do hope to build one next year, but in the meantime we are meeting in the back of one of the stores on Sunday mornings and evenings."

"I see." He slipped his wallet back in his coat pocket. "Then perhaps later you will accept a small token of my appreciation. Believe me, I never forget a favor."

A favor? Jenny considered the word for a moment. She hadn't thought of their helping Clint as a *favor*.

"We were glad to be of assistance," she smiled. "I only hope that Clint won't be too angry with me. I realize I did a very rash thing in contacting you, particularly when I know it was Clint's wish to manage on his own. But he just seemed so . . . helpless," she looked at Calvin Kincaid, her eyes troubled.

"Young lady, you did exactly the right thing. Clint is very proud, as you have learned; perhaps far too proud to accept help when it's needed. Let me assure you that I appreciate your deep concern for him. I believe, in time, Clint will come to appreciate you, as well."

The voice softened, and a thoughtful expression passed over the older man's face. Then, nodding again, he clamped his top-hat on his head and hurried out the door.

Jenny stared after him, puzzled. She could only wonder at the meaning of his last words.

Jenny tossed and turned through a sleepless night, her mind replaying the events of the past few days until sleep was impossible. Had Mr. Kincaid located Clint, she wondered? Or had Clint reclaimed his horse and galloped out of Cripple Creek forever?

He could no longer work his claim without the necessary funds. If he had not stayed at one of the hotels, then where had he gone? Was he spending a cold night in some abandoned miner's shack?

Though she had known him only four days, she felt a void in her life. Amazingly, it seemed much longer to her, partly because she had devoted every hour to caring for Clint. Now he was gone, and she was left with a fluttering heart and a bittersweet memory.

She rolled over again, clamping her eyelids together in an attempt to count sheep, hoping to lull herself to sleep. But Clint's blue eyes peered at her through a dark veil of semi-consciousness. No matter how many times she told herself that her emotional involvement stemmed from the protective attitude she had developed during her brief nursing period, she knew this was not wholly true.

If she were to be honest with herself, she would have to admit that Clint Kincaid had *almost* stolen her heart. Then, like a thief, he had retreated at the first sound of alarm. She felt he had sensed his effect on her and quickly vanished from her life.

Her eyes wide open again, she watched the night sky fade to a pale gray dawn. She could not free herself of the deep sense of loss. Then she buried her face in the pillow.

Jenny paused before the Palace Hotel where a raucous crowd lined the street, anticipating the arrival of the Florissant stage coach.

"Here she comes," someone yelled.

Jenny dashed to the edge of the crowd, eager to witness the dramatic arrival of the long-awaited stage as it rounded a bend in the road.

Dirt flew beneath the pounding hooves of six white horses as the driver curled a whip over the horses heads and turned down the main street. Pedestrians scattered for safety.

Shouts of excitement rang through the crowd, and for the first time all day, Jenny's spirits lifted. Her eyes focused on the distant driver as he leaned back in the seat, wrestling the reins in an effort to control the wildly-galloping horses. Then the squeal of brake shoes filled the air, and the stage jerked to a screeching halt before the crowded hotel.

Jenny leaned against the post of the electric arc light, glancing curiously at the bedraggled passengers stepping down. Their faces were flushed, their hats atilt, their eyes unnaturally bright after their breakneck plunge into Cripple Creek.

Jenny smiled as the passengers walked into the hotel on wobbly legs and turned inquisitive eyes back to the driver. The spreading grin in his heavily-bearded face confirmed his flair for a grand entrance.

Then, remembering her errand for Maude, she whirled and almost collided with the broad chest of a man in a patched buckskin jacket.

"Clint . . .," she whispered, unable to believe her eyes.

CHAPTER 5

THE SUDDEN MOVEMENT BESIDE CLINT drew Jenny's attention to his companion, and suddenly her blood froze in her veins.

The woman wore a ruffled dress of red satin, with an embarrasing display of cleavage. Her face was heavily layered with rouge, and bright auburn curls were piled in layers on top of her head. Her narrow green eyes held an icy glitter.

Jenny felt the blood creeping to her cheeks as she realized that this woman was a saloon girl—perhaps worse. She whirled back to Clint, her violet eyes darkening to deep purple pools. The smile on her lips had faded.

"Hello, Miss Townley," Clint's voice had sharpened to a razor's edge. "Running your little errands, I see."

"Yes," she mumbled, attempting to sidestep him.

His arm shot out, the strong hand gripping her shoulder. She nearly cried out from the hard pressure of his lean fingers, but she bit her lip, determined not to act like a frightened child.

"How dare you call my father!" he snarled.

Jenny stared at him, searching her mind for an explanation. The only reply she could give was the truth.

"I was worried about you."

The auburn-haired woman beside them laughed and snuggled closer to Clint.

"Who on earth is *she*, darlin'?"

Clint ignored the question and continued to grip Jenny's arm.

"I assume he paid you well." His tone was bitter. "Money is usually behind betrayal."

The words pierced her heart as nothing ever had. For a moment, her small face paled. Then a swift anger surged through her.

"All I wanted from your father was help for *you*!" she retorted, her voice trembling. "I never expected anything else. And I certainly never took anything from him!"

Clint glared at her, weighing her words for timeless seconds. Then he tightened his grip on her arm. "Sure!" he snorted.

Jenny tossed her head back and regarded him with new understanding. Suddenly she didn't know this man standing before her. Perhaps she never had. "I really don't care what you believe any more," she said, quietly. "Now, if you will get out of my path . . . ."

A look of surprise crossed Clint's face and he released her.

With all the dignity she could summon, Jenny turned and walked away, ignoring the raking stare that she knew followed her.

Halfway home, her strength gave way and her eyes filled with hot, stinging tears. But even that angered her. *He isn't worth my tears*, she thought, determined to blink away the moisture. She had been mistaken about Clint Kincaid, she told herself. He was not the man she had thought he was, and with that knowledge she could forget him.

The image of the gaudy woman intruded on her thoughts, and she shuddered. If that was the kind of woman Clint preferred, then she was glad to have discovered it now. She would never, ever think of him again.

She was still repeating those words to herself when she burst through the door of her cabin. Maude's sack, which she had completely forgotten to deliver, was still in her arms. She placed it on the table and removed her cloak.

Her father turned from where he was bent over the fireplace, shoveling ashes into a bucket and met her eyes as she joined him. "What's wrong, daughter?"

"I suppose I'm tired from the walk," she replied.

"Calvin Kincaid was here while you were in town," he said, turning back to his work. He shoveled the last of the ashes into the bucket.

In spite of her determination, curiosity won out over her vow to separate herself from the Kincaids.

"What did he say?"

"He located his son," Joseph paused, laying the small shovel across the bucket. "It seems that Clint will not accept his help—or his money."

Jenny nodded, glancing absently at the fireplace. "I know. I just saw Clint in town. He is so angry with me, Father . . . ."

Joseph nodded. "I suppose we could expect that

kind of reaction from a man as independent as Clint. But I imagine in time he will realize that you were only trying to help."

"I doubt it! I just can't understand his suspicion and distrust. We were good to him. We cared for him when he was hurt . . ." Her words, like her thoughts, wandered aimlessly. Then suddenly she remembered that her father had not heard the conversation or seen Clint with the . . . other woman. "And besides, he is no gentlemen," she added lamely. Then, for no reason, the memory of his kiss filled her mind, overpowering all he had said and done to hurt her.

"I think, Jennifer, that Clint has some fine qualities, despite everything," her father replied slowly. "He is merely cursed with an overdose of hard-headedness—something he will have to come to terms with on his own. Perhaps the hard lesson of experience is all that will alter his strong will." He gave Jenny an encouraging smile. "Calvin Kincaid loves his son enough to give him time to find himself. He has asked us to try to persuade Clint to take the envelope of money he left here for him—if we see him again, that is."

"Money?" Jenny gasped. "He won't take any money, Father. Do you think you should have agreed to keep it for him?"

Joseph shrugged. "I am a father, too. I could not refuse to help. Besides, Clint may change his mind. But I do believe he will have to undergo a drastic change first—before he accepts help from *anyone*. "

"Well, *I* won't be interfering in his life again. I can assure you of that!"

Joseph smiled tenderly at his daughter. Then he stood and carefully lifted the bucket of ashes. "What about Maude's sack?" he asked, glancing toward the kitchen. "Why don't you take it over and stay for a visit?"

Jenny nodded. "Yes, I need a good laugh—and I can always count on Maude for that!"

CHAPTER 6

A GOSSAMER VEIL OF SMOKE drifted up from the
cookfires of the mining camps along the Pikes Peak
foothills. Jenny gripped the seat of the buckboard as
her father guided the horses up the bumpy road to yet
another mining site. Many times Jenny had glanced up
into these hills and wondered about the miners—
particularly in the evenings when the glow of their
kerosene lamps lit the hillside like a thousand fireflies.

She had wondered about the men in these camps,
men who struggled and dreamed and froze to death,
hoping to wrest their bonanza from the grudging
earth.

And now she was seeing them at work, twisting a
windlass to haul up chunks of rock, swinging a heavy
pick over brawny shoulders, pulling on gear to climb
down into a freshly-dug cavern. Each had that
unmistakable gleam in his eye, kindled by the burning
desire for riches. Jenny had seen that gleam in Clint's
eyes when he spoke of his mining claim on the first
night he had come to their cabin.

The buckboard struck another bump and Jenny's thoughts swung back to the ride. Despite the roughness of the roads, Jenny was enjoying this outing with her father. After the hard cold winter, the hot sun on her face was a feeling to be savored. She glanced down at her blue muslin dress, where particles of dust were already gathering on the full skirt. She decided she didn't mind the dirt either; a bright spring day in the high country was worth any price. As she approached her first summer in Cripple Creek, she could only pray it would not be as short as the locals predicted.

"Whoa!" her father called to the horses as they entered the mining area.

Although her father had been delivering supplies to the mining camps for weeks, this was the first time Jenny had joined him. She studied the camp with growing interest. Mining tools, ropes, and massive wooden buckets were scattered about the wooden shaft. Several workers turned to regard them with undisguised interest.

Her father waved to them and jumped down from the wagon. "Good morning, gentlemen!"

Many of the miners already knew her father. At his approach, they made a swipe for their slouch hats and bowed respectfully.

"Mornin', Reverend," several deep voices boomed.

This camp, like the last one, eagerly awaited the delivery of much-needed supplies from Warren and Williams grocery. Jenny glanced at the men's lean, whiskered faces, wondering how long it had been since they had enjoyed a decent meal.

At a comfortable distance from the work site,

crude, one-room shacks appeared to have been tossed up overnight, some still in the final stages of completion. Yet, this mining site was more advanced than the one they had just left, where picks, shovels, and gold pans were flung carelessly beside canvas tents. And in front of the tents, a frying pan and coffeepot had rested on a huge, smooth rock. Seeing their "kitchen" had given Jenny a new appreciation for her own.

Despite the intense morning sun, she shivered involuntarily, imagining their struggle to survive the Colorado winters in those tents, or in the crude structures where cracks in the logs were visible even from a distance.

Conscious of the sweeping stares and sudden hush of the shuffling men, Jenny suddenly recalled Clint's warning that a mining area was not a safe place for a lady. How ridiculous! And why did she care what he said, anyway? He was probably judging everyone by his own standards.

Her eyes crept over the group of strangers and an odd disappointment filled her. She would never admit that some part of her searched for Clint . . . still.

Somehow, she had half expected to find him at one of the mining sites. No doubt, he had left Cripple Creek, after all.

Before that thought had fully crystallized, a hoarse cry in the distance sent everyone scurrying for shelter.

"Get down in the buckboard!" her father yelled.

"What?" she gasped, her eyes scanning the miners who ran for shelter.

"Fire!" came the cry again, and just as she dropped onto the dusty floorboard, the hillside trembled with an ear-splitting blast. The sound exploded in her eardrums, echoing through her taut body like a drum, magnified a thousandfold.

Her hands had automatically flown to cover her ears, and her lids were squeezed together in fear. But the blast soon died away in a reverberating echo, and she felt a gentle hand tapping her shoulder.

"Don't be afraid, Jenny. They're just blasting over at the next site. I should have warned you."

"Yeah, that's Shorty over at the Isabell!" another voice yelled. "We've gotten used to dodging his rocks! He sets off a stick of dynamite two or three times a day. Reckon by now our ears are numb. But I guess it's pretty scary for a lady."

Jenny turned toward the voice, her bonnet, knocked askew, framing one violet eye. The bearded young man standing beside the wagon looked her over with obvious admiration.

Fortunately, at that moment, he was distracted by several miners who had appeared to help unload the supplies from the back of the wagon, and he turned away to lend a hand. She climbed quickly back into the seat and adjusted her bonnet.

"What's going on in town, Reverend?" someone yelled.

"Well, let's see. Willis McGhee had too much firewater at the Red Garter yesterday," he responded. "Somebody put him on his horse and headed him for home, but he said he wasn't finished yet and turned around and jumped his horse right through the window!"

A roar went up from the crowd. Apparently her father seemed intent on rectifying any notions that a minister was stiff and prudish. Moreover, he had a knack with the men, Jenny thought, a penchant for putting them at ease, making them feel he was one of them.

Before long he had climbed back into the wagon. "See you next week," Joseph called.

"Bring your purty daughter again, Reverend!"

Jenny's cheeks colored beneath the miners' scrutiny, but she turned to smile at them as her father slapped the reins and the buckboard bounced over the rutted trail.

"Now where?" Jenny asked.

"Just one more stop," her father replied, guiding his horses up the narrow road that snaked deeper into the hills.

As they jostled over yet another mudhole, a dull ache settled into the muscles of Jenny's lower back. She tried to divert her mind from the pain, knowing it would be hours before they returned to the comfort of their cabin.

She would at least be more comfortable without her hair tightly pinned into a chignon at the back of her head. It was simply too hot and too long a ride to be unnecessarily concerned with propriety. She untied the strings of her bonnet and reached up to free her hair from the restraining pins.

Soon the silky strands of raven hair flew freely about her face, fanned by the breeze.

A deep sigh of contentment slipped from her lips. She leaned back, enjoying the golden sunlight, the tangy smell of evergreen and woodsmoke, the exhilarating sense of freedom.

She glanced about her with interest. This was a strange and beautiful land, requiring a special kind of strength for those who claimed it. She loved it here, despite the hardships and adverse weather . . . despite the memories of Clint Kincaid.

She would not think of him, she resolved, consciously focusing on another topic. "Cripple Creek," she repeated the name. "Isn't that an odd name for a gold camp?"

"Surely you've heard the story," her father laughed. "Long before Mr. Womack struck the El Paso Lode, this place had been christened. The first settlers who passed through felt that it had decidedly 'crippled' their progress."

Jenny threw back her head and laughed. How she enjoyed her father! Thus pleasantly occupied, she paid little attention at first to the small windowless hut they were approaching.

Then, as they drew closer, she leaned forward curiously.

"Who lives there, Father?"

"I'm not sure," he replied, slowing the horses as they drew nearer.

The door opened and a tall, lean man strolled out. *Clint!*

Jenny's breath lodged in her throat. "Father!" she whirled around. "Did you know Clint Kincaid lived here?"

Joseph leaned back in the wagon, tugging at the reins. "No, but I guess I shouldn't be surprised. I knew his mining site was just over that hill. Good morning, Clint!" he called out.

Jenny immediately began fidgeting with her bonnet strings, desperately wishing she had not unpinned her hair. She sat rigid, and would have preferred to dive into the floorboard rather than face him. But it was too late.

She lifted her chin and turned her gaze upon him. Immediately, she could feel her mouth dropping open as she stared, shocked by the change in his appearance. The unkempt, gaunt man scarcely resembled the Clint Kincaid of a month ago. Suddenly all the anger melted away and her heart was stabbed with pity. He looked like a shadow of the man she had known.

His searching look traveled over her, and focused almost absently on the soft flow of dark hair about her face. For a moment she thought she caught an expression of regret in his hollow eyes.

"Clint, could we talk for a minute?" Joseph asked.

Clint shoved his hands deep into the pockets of his patched trousers, and approached the wagon.

"Reverend Townley," he nodded. "How have you been?"

"Can't complain, Clint, but I must confess our concern for you has kept us worried. Is your wound healing properly?"

Automatically, Clint's hand slipped up to the front of his flannel shirt. "It's healing, but I don't know how properly."

Joseph reached into his coat pocket and withdrew a large envelope. "I believe this belongs to you." He extended the envelope.

Clint frowned. "I don't understand."

"Your father left it for you. I think he wants to have a small stake in your mining operation. If you're as smart as I think you are, you'll take it."

Jenny stared at her father. She had always thought of him as a quiet, retiring man who tended to his own business and allowed others to do the same. Yet, there were times when he assumed an undisputed authority. This was one of those times.

Clint studied the envelope.

"The money is yours, Clint," Joseph said firmly. "Take it."

Slowly he reached for the envelope, then hesitated.

"I'll take it . . . but only because he has given me a way to repay him," Clint said roughly. "I'll make him a partner in the mine, and I'll take his money as collateral. As soon as we strike, he'll get every cent back. And we will strike!" The thought brought new luster to his eyes.

Jenny watched his fingers close over the envelope and felt herself breathing a relieved sigh. Clint Kincaid was the stubbornest man she had ever met. If he was willing to meet his father halfway, there was hope yet.

"We're delivering groceries for Warren and Williams," her father continued. "Do you need anything today?"

Clint turned and sauntered curiously to the back of the wagon. "Maybe a few staples," he replied casually.

"Take what you need and we'll figure the bill."

Watching Clint ponder the items, Jenny could not restrain the tenderness that filled her. No doubt he was half-starved. His pride had cost him dearly.

Clint selected a few sacks and a tin of coffee. "This will be all," he said, hoisting the items for inspection. "How much do I owe you?"

Joseph checked the list of supplies and quickly figured the amount on the bottom of his tablet, which he showed Clint. With a sigh of resignation, Clint opened the envelope and extracted a few bills.

"Thank you, Reverend Townley."

"Take care of yourself, Clint," Joseph smiled. "And if you happen to be in Cripple Creek on

Sunday, we'd be mighty proud to have you worship with us. We meet in the back of Warren and Williams grocery. Nothing fancy—but we get the week started off right."

Clint glanced at Jenny, then smiled at Joseph. "Thank you, sir. I'll consider that."

"Well, good day." Joseph tapped the reins and the horses lunged forward.

Jenny dared not glance over her shoulder, yet she sensed Clint's lingering stare upon them. He had not even spoken to her, and yet, despite her resolve to forget him, she was happier than she had been in days.

The members of the small congregation were heartily singing "Bringing in the Sheaves" when Clint slipped quietly into the back row and took his seat on one of the wooden benches.

Jenny, dressed in a new gown of green muslin, tried to keep her attention on the hymnbook, while her mind struggled with the reality of Clint actually attending their worship service. Her lips, however, moved mechanically over the words long committed to memory, and freed her eyes for an uncontrollable glance in his direction.

It was Clint, all right, dressed in a dark gray suit and starched white shirt. He towered above the crowd, his golden hair neatly combed, his freshly shaven face still thin, yet disturbingly handsome. His blue eyes caught hers, and he smiled at her. Then he reached out and grasped an open hymnal.

Mesmerized by the sight, Jenny lost her place in the song. Her eyes widened as his rich baritone voice suddenly filled the small room.

Jenny smiled, her heart leaping with joy. The words appeared to be as familiar to Clint as to anyone else in the room. With renewed hope, she forced her eyes back to the hymnal, her voice ringing out once again.

After the service, the crowd milled about, enjoying the company of friends. Clint lingered in the back row. Jenny could feel his gaze was upon her as she greeted those friends who had been sitting next to her.

Although she had not expected him to attend the service, Jenny had taken special care in choosing her outfit that morning. The fashionable puff sleeves and molded waist of the green dress accentuated her slim figure. The toes of her black kid heels peeped from beneath the wide-flaring hem, and a velvet, brimless toque crowned her dark, upswept curls.

Jenny was conscious of Clint's eyes following her every move as she placed her hymnbook into a box by the podium. Then, ignoring Myrtle Tubbs' hawkish glare, Jenny moved gracefully down the narrow aisle that separated the rows of wooden benches and greeted Clint.

"Good morning! Nice to have you with us today!" She smiled at him trying to sound casual, though her heart was racing.

"Thank you." Clint bowed politely. His tailored suit was apparently new, and it fit him to perfection.

"Good morning, Clint." Joseph walked up at that moment.

"Sir." Clint shook the proffered hand. "I enjoyed your message."

"Delighted that you came."

Clint glanced around the dispersing crowd. "Reverend Townley, I'd like to invite you and Jennifer to have lunch with me at one of the hotels."

Joseph was silent for a moment. Then he turned to Jenny. "You go with Mr. Kincaid, Jenny. I am meeting with a few of the parishoners shortly and will take lunch at home afterward."

"You see," Clint grinned a challenge, "now you have no excuse."

Jenny opened her mouth to protest, but her father insisted. "It will be good for you to get out of the kitchen for a spell."

"Well . . . all right," she smiled at Clint.

As Joseph turned to speak to someone in the aisle, Jenny led the way through the narrow door that connected the small meeting room with the front of the grocery store. The large room was unusually quiet with no customers milling about, or old-timers swapping tales before the pot-bellied stove.

Clint leaned around Jenny to press the latch on the heavy door. As they stepped out into the sparkling June sunshine, Clint's hand slipped protectively around her elbow, guiding her over the uneven boardwalk.

Automatically, Jenny glanced down the street to the corner where she had seen Clint . . . and that woman. She would never have believed, then, that she would be so quick to forgive him for his cruel behavior. But, of course, according to Scripture, a Christian was *supposed* to forgive and forget. And seeing Clint, so ragged and pathetic that day at his mining site had reduced her anger to pity.

"I'm glad you came to church today," she looked at Clint. And you have a marvelous voice! I had no idea—"

"That I could sing? Or that I could sing a hymn?"

"Both!" she laughed.

"What would you say if I told you that I was reared in a church?" he asked, steering her around a group of miners who stood before the bathhouse. "As a matter of fact, I sang in the choir that my mother directed, and my father is a church elder."

Jenny's mouth dropped open, then she clamped her lips together and nodded reflectively. "Somehow I would say I'm not surprised."

"You see, Jenny, I'm the proverbial black sheep," he admitted, his tone more serious. "That's why it was so hard for me to face my father."

"Clint," she turned to face him, "I apologize for intruding into your private life. I had no right to do that."

He stared down at the boardwalk for a moment then looked at her with a wry grin. "Actually, now I'm glad that you did interfere. You made it easier for us to settle our differences. Jenny, I'm a stubborn man. You know that, don't you?"

"Well . . . yes. But we all have our faults."

He threw back his head and laughed. "I certainly do! I have strayed quite far from my religious upbringing, and from the laws of the God I've always worshiped. That's why I objected to coming to church with you. But," he glanced at her thoughtfully, "I realized that long before today. I am sorry."

"Do you mean that, Clint?"

"I mean it, but don't expect a miracle overnight. For the past year, I've lived a rather sinful life. Getting right with God and man is going to take time and patience."

"I am a very patient woman," she smiled. And then she realized it was happening to her again—that same crazy joy that filled her whenever she was near him. But, now, for the first time, she dared hope, too.

"Clint," Jenny frowned, hesitating to ask yet unable to resist, "has there been any news of Benson?"

"None. The Sheriff hasn't found him. He even wired St. Louis, but there's been no word." He paused, thinking. "Our paths may cross again someday. And when that happens, I'll settle the score myself."

"Clint, please don't take the law in your own hands. I'm certain the man will be apprehended in time. Try to forget what he did."

"I'm to turn the other cheek, is that it?" The old bitterness had crept back into the intense blue eyes. "I told you, Jenny, don't expect any quick miracles!"

She was glad when they reached the hotel. The conversation had suddenly become unpleasant, and she wished she had never mentioned Benson.

Clint ushered her through the lobby of the hotel, where a huge fireplace still held the embers of the evening fire. When summer evenings turned cool, miners and businessmen gathered together here, discussing the best methods of marketing their gold.

The elegance of the dining room brought a gasp of surprise, as Jenny stared at the brocade wallpaper, the cut crystal chandelier, and the gleaming table service. It was the first time Jenny had taken a meal here at the popular hotel, and she glanced at Clint with appreciation.

"When are you returning to your mine?" she asked after the efficient waiter seated them, took their order, and served them.

"This afternoon. I've hired a couple of men to help me and," he hesitated, then grinned, "with the financial assistance of my new partner, I have purchased better equipment. I wonder now, how I could have been so bullheaded when my father offered to help.''

He lifted the china cup to his lips and sipped his coffee. ''I want to tell you something, Jenny. I wrote a long letter to my father, thanking him for his investment. I made it very clear that I would accept his money on one condition: that his attorneys draw up a legal document to give him a fifty percent share of the mine. I hope he agrees to that, since I've already spent some of the money. But he won't regret it,'' he added with conviction. ''I intend to make us both rich.''

Jenny's smile faded. Wealth seemed much too important to Clint. Ambition was admirable, she reasoned, as long as it did not become an obsession.

''I'm enjoying my meal,'' she speared a silver fork into the golden chicken breast. She did not want to dwell on negative thoughts now. Whatever doubts hovered in her mind could be dealt with later.

''I'm glad,'' he smiled. ''You work so hard for your father, and for everyone else. You deserve to have others waiting on you for a change.''

''I would be bored to death in no time,'' she laughed, glancing in the direction of a loud voice across the room. The voice belonged to a swaggering man who was arguing with a waiter. Beside him stood a red-headed woman . . . the woman she had seen with Clint!

''Wonder what Kate is up to?'' Clint said, glancing at the couple.

The food had suddenly turned to stone in Jenny's mouth. While she had not dared mention the subject of the questionable redhead, she had wondered many times about the woman.

She could not resist another glance in that direction. The woman was dressed in black—a more modestly designed gown than before. Yet, her make-up was overdone, and her haughty expression had not changed.

"You're wondering why I was with her that day," Clint read her thoughts.

Jenny could not look at him. She sat toying with the handle of her cup, hating the blush that stained her cheeks.

"I've known Kate all my life." He leaned back in the chair, glancing toward the door through which the couple had just departed.

Jenny's head jerked up in surprise.

"She's from Denver," he explained. "Born and raised near my folks' home. But something happened to her a few years back," he sighed. "The man she was engaged to left town quite unexpectedly. Kate believes her father bought him off, since the family never approved of him. I had heard that she moved to Cripple Creek, but I had forgotten until I ran into her on the street one day. She's the friend I referred to at the hotel, but she helped me get my own room on credit."

He paused, studying Jenny's startled face.

"Contrary to what you may have imagined about me," he continued, "I could never patronize Kate in her new lifestyle. Perhaps someday she'll come to her senses."

"Oh, Clint, I hope so," Jenny responded sadly, thinking about the 'ladies of the night' who had flocked to Cripple Creek with the gold rush. Her thoughts returned to Kate and, realizing she had no reason to be jealous, she suddenly felt compassion for

81

her. "I'd like to get to know Kate," she said on an impulse.

"That's good of you, Jenny. But if you were to be seen with Kate, the town gossips would slash you to shreds."

"I don't care! If people are too proud to help someone in need, then they had better check the condition of their souls, as well."

"How true!" He nodded, as an amused grin tilted his lips. "You're quite a lady! And though I agree with your father that you should be in a more proper environment, I am glad that you're in Cripple Creek."

"You also accused me of being too self-righteous for any man," her eyes sparkled with humor.

He chuckled. "So I did. But I've mellowed since those days when I was bitter and sick, sprawled before your fireplace. Maybe I've decided to toss my hat in the ring with the other bachelors of Cripple Creek."

She was conscious of a waiter hovering at their table, anxious to accommodate them with dessert.

' "No more for me." She pushed her plate aside. "I cannot eat another bite." As the waiter disappeared, she turned back to Clint. "When will you be back in town?"

"Next weekend," a large grin spread over his face. "In fact, your father may get tired of turning me from his doorstep."

Jenny laughed softly. "You're in luck, Clint Kincaid. My father never turns anyone from our doorstep."

"Luck is not the word, dear lady. Meeting you is one of the greatest blessings of my life!"

"Why, thank you," she gasped.

"Perhaps God had something to do with it, after all." He was more serious than she had seen him all day.

"Yes," she whispered, remembering the prayer she had so earnestly prayed on the night Clint left her cabin without a goodbye. "Clint, I prayed I would see you again."

Clint stared at her. Then he rose quickly. "We had best be going," he said. "I have to go check on some things, and—"

"Yes, of course," she responded as he held her chair, but inwardly she felt a sudden stab. Was his interest in her only important where spiritual matters were concerned? She wanted to help him, of course, but more than that she wanted to love him and for him to love her. Perhaps that was expecting too much.

CHAPTER 7

SUMMER CAME AT LAST to Cripple Creek. On summer nights in the high altitude, the moon was an enormous silver disk suspended in space. At times Jenny felt she could almost reach out into the star-spangled heavens and touch that moon. Was it the altitude that gave her such a sensation, she wondered, or was it the fact that she was spending time with with Clint?

Clint Kincaid came to Cripple Creek every weekend . After the worship service on Sundays, the two would lunch at one of the hotels, or pack a picnic basket and hike up to a favorite alpine meadow beside a mountain stream. Beneath Clint's attentive care, Jenny thrived like a columbine in the mountain meadow, lifting its delicate face to the Rocky Mountain sun.

"Jenny, these past weeks have been the happiest of my life," Clint said to her one soft summer evening as they strolled away from a restaurant on Bennett Avenue. "I seem to have found peace again. And even though I haven't struck gold, I believe there's a rich vein of ore in my mine. I *know* it's there," he amended.

"Hello, Clint!"

The sharp female voice stopped them at the street corner, and they turned to face Kate, dressed in flashy, black satin. Her face was heavily rouged, and the green eyes were dull and lifeless.

"Hello, Kate." Clint's tone was reserved. "How have you been?"

"Just dandy." She tossed her head back, and the braided red curls shimmered in the glow of the street lamp. "I see you're back with your proper little friend." She cast a harsh look at Jenny's modest blue gown and matching toque.

"Kate, this is Jennifer Townley," Clint said. "Jennifer, Kate McClain. Jennifer's father is Joseph Townley, the minister from St. Louis."

"Whoopee!" Kate lifted her ruby nails in a gesture of disdain.

"Hello, Kate." Jenny extended her hand, ignoring the woman's bad manners.

"I don't shake hands with women," Kate snarled, turning back to Clint. "What have you been doing? I haven't seen you in a while." The false confidence in her tone slipped away, and now her voice flattened to a hollow, almost desperate sound.

"I'm staying at the mining camp most of the time," he replied. "Except for Sundays, when I go to hear the Reverend Townley. You should try church yourself, Kate. It might surprise you."

Kate bristled at the invitation. "I don't need any prissy Sunday sermons!" She whirled and charged down the street, turning into the swinging door of the Lucky Dollar.

Clint and Jenny stared after her, then Clint slipped his hand through Jenny's arm and they walked in silence back up the hill to her cabin.

"It's sad to see such desperation in a person's face," Jenny finally said.

Clint nodded. "Unfortunately, she sees no need to change. And she's suspicious of anyone who tries to help her."

"Do her parents know. . ." she faltered, searching for words, "what she does here?"

"They're the last she'd want to know," he said, as they reached Jenny's walkway. "They're stern and unrelenting. I don't think they ever really tried to understand Kate."

They paused at the doorstep and Jenny tilted her head to the brilliant moon. "I wish I could help her," she said quietly. "Maybe in time I can. What do you think?"

"I think you're beautiful in the moonlight."

She looked up at him. In the beginning, Jenny had felt shy and awkward with Clint. But as she surrendered to the knowledge that she was in love with him, a new kind of courage filled her heart. She had a deep and certain assurance that she would never love like this again, and she was determined to win his heart, if possible.

Clint clasped both her hands in his and lifted her fingertips to his lips. Neither felt the need for words as they stared deeply into each other's eyes. A whisper of a sigh slipped from her lips as Clint's arms tightened around her shoulders and his lips dipped to claim hers. A sweet and tender yearning filled her senses, and she had an insane wish that this moment would never end.

Clint released her slowly and stepped back still holding her hand. She realized, suddenly, that his large hand was beginning to tremble.

"Jenny. Oh, Jenny." He shook his head, the blue eyes reflecting the glow of the moon as he stared at her. "I don't know what I'm going to do about you."

"Whatever do you mean?"

"I don't know. I'm not sure." He shook his head again, as he dropped her hands. "But each time I leave you, it's harder to say goodbye."

"Goodbye only until the weekend," she reminded him. "The church picnic is Saturday afternoon, and I'm baking my famous caramel cake. You don't want to miss that, do you?"

"I'd never forgive myself!" he teased, quickly kissing her cheek. "See you then," he called as he turned and walked off down the hill to the hotel, where he spent his weekends. Jenny's loving eyes followed the tall, broad-shouldered frame. There was a kind of superior confidence about Clint Kincaid, as though he knew exactly what he wanted and was determined to get it. At the same time, Jenny sensed an inner restlessness that she knew only God could quiet.

What did Clint really want? She thought, staring into the darkness. Gold, of course; he wanted to discover gold to prove to himself, or perhaps to his father, that he could succeed where so many others had failed.

"Well, maybe someday you'll want me just as badly, Clint Kincaid," she whispered hopefully. "And until then, I'll just have to pray for patience!"

The next afternoon, Jenny and members of her Sunday school class, were delivering New Testaments to patients at the Sisters of Mercy Hospital. The New Testaments had been sent by their home church in St. Louis to be dispensed where needed. Jenny and the women had decided to begin at the hospital.

Jenny glanced into one crowded ward, then came to an abrupt halt. A tangled mass of red hair fanned out on a pillow, framing a still, deathly-pale face.

Jenny clutched the sleeve of a passing nurse. "What's wrong with her?" She pointed to Kate.

"Took an overdose of laudanum. But she's going to be all right," the Sister smiled.

Jenny slipped to the bed to stare down at the sick woman. Without the make-up and with her eyes closed, Kate seemed younger than Jenny imagined. Now she guessed her to be only in her mid-twenties, although harsh lines were already faintly etched on her pale skin.

Suddenly, the dark lashes fluttered open, and as recognition dawned, the red head turned, and Kate fixed a blank stare on the far wall.

"Hello, Kate." Jenny's hand gently pressed the arm beneath the crisp white sheet. "I'm so sorry . . ." she said softly, ". . . about your trouble. Maybe you think no one cares about you, but you're wrong. I care." The red head tossed on the pillow, and green eyes shot sparks of hatred.

"What kind of idiot are you?" Her voice was a mere whisper. "Why should you care about me?"

Jenny hesitated, carefully choosing her words. "Because underneath all the anger and hatred, I believe you're a good person."

Tears sparkled in the green eyes and the drawn

mouth began to tremble. "Go away." She turned back to the wall.

"I'll go if you want me to, but I wish you would believe that I want to be your friend."

Kate turned to stare at her. "What are you—some kind of martyr?"

"No," Jenny shook her head. "I just believe that we are put on this earth for a purpose. I've always felt my purpose was to help other people. I'd like to help you—if you'll let me."

"What could you possibly do for me?"

"I could listen. Sometimes when problems seem too great to bear, it helps to have someone who'll just listen." Jenny hesitated, waiting for a response. Kate merely stared at her. "And I want to give you this." She reached down into her basket and withdrew a New Testament. "You may have read one before, but if you haven't, perhaps it will help to know about a Man who died on a cross for our sins—my sins, your sins, everyone's sins. There is no sin so ugly that it cannot be forgiven." Jenny spoke slowly, hoping the message would penetrate the woman's protective shell.

A nurse hovered in the background, waiting to administer medication.

"I'll go now." Jenny stepped back from the bed. "But I'll be back later in the week."

Something surfaced in Kate's green eyes, a look of pain or need. Jenny suspected that the woman was too proud to respond. Still, the New Testament was gripped firmly in her thin hands, and feeling that she could do no more, Jenny slipped from the ward.

When Jenny returned on Thursday, Kate was sitting up in bed, combing the tangled ends of her thick, red hair. Her face was fresh and clean, and she was wearing a becoming bedjacket.

"Kate!" Jenny gasped. "You're much prettier without all the rouge." Jenny bit her lip, fearing she had angered the woman with her outburst, but Kate's expression was almost pleasant. "I shouldn't have said that," Jenny apologized, "but your skin is fair and soft, and with those lovely features, you don't need powder and paint," she added, pulling up a chair.

Kate shrugged. "It's become a habit. Others wear it. I see you don't," the green eyes inspected Jenny, "but then I suppose you're perfect," she finished tartly.

"Oh no, I'm not!" Jenny laughed. "Kate, I was wondering if you'd like me to notify any of your family or friends about . . . that you've been sick,"

The thin brows arched derisively. "That I tried to kill myself, you mean?" The bitterness still edged her voice. "Nobody cares what I do with my life." She stared glumly into her hand mirror, then lifted the brush again to rake through one flaming strand of hair.

"I care," Jenny replied softly. "In fact, if you're out of the hospital by Saturday, I want to invite you to the church picnic. Clint and I will come get you."

Kate dropped the mirror and stared at Jenny. "You must live in some sort of dream world. You obviously have no idea what kind of trouble you'd be heaping on yourself, and Clint—and *me*. Why, those ladies at that church picnic would run screaming in horror if I showed up."

"No, they wouldn't. Love is what Christianity is all

about. Believe me, everyone will be glad to have you at the picnic."

Kate shook her head in disbelief. "I have tried very hard to hate you. Not because there's ever been anything between Clint and me—more's the pity. I like him—a lot. But he's just a friend. I guess I forgot about him when I said no one cared. Clint cares because he's a decent guy." Kate's green eyes darkened thoughtfully as she stared at Jenny. "From the moment I first saw you, I wanted to hate you; worked at it, in fact. Anyone can tell at a glance that you're a genuine lady. And that burned me, if you get what I mean. But as I get to know you, I think you may be the only real person I've ever known . . . . I don't understand you, Jenny," she said after a long pause. "How can you love everybody— especially someone like me. It just isn't normal."

Jenny shrugged, "I think love is the most normal thing in the world. God is love you know. And if He lives inside our hearts—well, we just can't help loving!" She frowned thoughtfully. "That doesn't mean I like everything a person does, but it doesn't keep me from liking the person, Kate." Jenny leaned closer, "Please say you'll come to the picnic with us. I promise you'll have a good time—and no one will run from you. You'll see."

Kate blinked at her, trying to comprehend this strange young woman. She shook her head. "If you want me to come, okay, I will." She smiled for the first time. "I think I'd like that."

"You've done what?" Clint shouted across Jenny's living room.

"I've invited Kate to come with us to the picnic," Jenny repeated.

Clint tossed his black felt hat on a chair and sauntered into the kitchen where Jenny was wrapping her cake in cheesecloth. He thrust his hands on the sides of his gray waistcoat and tilted his head in amazement.

"Jenny, I know you mean well," he said, struggling to regain his composure, "but this isn't going to work, believe me. Those ladies will have Kate's head on a platter. And if Kate loses that flaming temper of hers, your nice little church picnic could turn into a hair-pulling brawl! What does your father say?" He glanced around the cabin from which Joseph had just departed, taking the first load of picnic supplies.

"He's used to my outlandish ideas," Jenny teased. "Really, Clint, this doesn't seem so unusual to father. He's always been open-minded." A tiny frown puckered her smooth brow, "I'm disappointed that you aren't willing to look on the positive side, too. I've included Kate in our prayers at the Wednesday night prayer service. So it won't be a surprise to the ladies when they see her at the picnic with us."

"With us?" Clint moaned, pressing his palm to his forehead.

"Stop worrying. Everything will be fine. Now will you help me pack the picnic basket? Father will soon be back with the wagon. Then we'll go to the hotel and pick up Kate and be on our way to Mt. Pisgah."

"Jenny, you're asking for trouble. But I'm game." Clint reached for the cake, a reluctant grin pulling his lips. "At least this will be anything but dull!"

Kate was dressed in a modest, black dress with lace collar and cuffs. The rouge and thick makeup were conspicuously absent, and her mane of red hair had been subdued into a sleek chignon, secured with a diamond clasp, her only ornament. The expression in her bright green eyes was guarded, almost shy.

"You look beautiful!" Jenny called as Joseph helped Kate into the wagon.

"Thank you." Kate glanced self-consciously at Jenny and Clint, seated on a quilt in the back of the wagon. "Hello, Clint. And don't you dare say anything."

"Not even that I'm pleased you're coming?" he asked with a grin. "Seriously, Kate, I am pleased."

"Well, the afternoon isn't over yet," she countered, pressing the wide hem of her broadcloth dress in place, as she settled onto the front seat.

"Kate, you look much more proper than I do." Jenny lifted a hand to retie the ribbon that scarcely restrained the mass of dark hair tumbling down her back. Her cotton dress was bright and colorful.

"Both of our ladies are lovely," Joseph smiled reassuringly, seating himself at the front of the wagon. "It's going to be a good day."

When they arrived at the picnic site, the women were fussing over the food, while the men clustered about Little Joe Hammond, who was tuning his violin. The happy mood of the crowd was manifest in the lilting voices and pleasant faces.

Those pleasant faces turned to the approaching wagon, and each registered a different form of shock. At the end of the table, Myrtle Tubbs' face reddened and the hawkish eyes threatened to burst from their sockets.

"Great day for a picnic," Joseph called to them as he yanked the horses to a halt.

A deathly hush had settled over the crowd of wide

eyes and open mouths. Suddenly one of the deacons regained control and bounded forward.

"Yes, it's a fine day, Reverend. Do you need any help with the food, Miss Jenny?"

"Could you get the basket for us?" Jenny asked as her glance slipped over the man's head to the knot of whispering people. "Hello, everyone!" she called out, a subtle challenge in her voice.

A reserved greeting rose from the group. Jenny's violet eyes traveled over each face, seeking their cooperation in an unspoken glance. One of the ladies walked up, extending her hand to Kate.

"We are so glad you could come today," she smiled.

"Thank you," Kate nodded stiffly, wary green eyes moving cautiously over the group.

"Well, strike up the instruments, gentlemen," Joseph called out. "The picnic is officially underway!"

A man tested his Jews' harp, as Little Joe tuned his violin, and soon the perky music had captured the attention of the crowd.

"Kate, will you give me a hand with the tablecloth?" Jenny smiled encouragingly.

"What can I do?" Clint asked, the blue eyes twinkling with humor. "If that fried chicken is as good as it smells, Jenny, there may be a fight over the last drumstick!"

"Surely everyone will remember his manners," she responded loudly, hoping the double meaning in her words would melt the crowd's reserve.

"I told you I shouldn't have come!" Kate muttered to Jenny. "They don't want me here."

"Nonsense!" Jenny replied lightly. "Everything is going to be just fine. You'll see."

One by one, the other women drifted up, offering Kate tentative smiles and words of welcome.

Myrtle Tubbs, meanwhile, struck a path to Joseph. "Could I speak with you privately, Reverend?" she asked, her voice as brittle as the dried twigs at their feet.

"Of course!" Joseph gave her his warmest smile. "I must say you're looking well today, Myrtle. This lovely August weather must be agreeing with you." He followed Myrtle to the edge of the crowd and took a deep strengthening breath.

"What's *not* agreeing with me is your guest!" Myrtle tossed her gray head back. Snapping, dark eyes attacked Joseph's pleasant face. "Reverend, I don't know what's gotten into you and your daughter! But I think it's an insult to the rest of us to bring people like that . . . that *woman* to our picnic!"

"Oh?" Joseph's dark brows arched in dismay. "Are we to exclude everyone who isn't already a member of the congregation, Myrtle?"

"Not *everyone* !" Myrtle hissed, "but a woman of her – her *profession* is not welcome among decent folk! I must say, I'm shocked at you, Reverend." Her tone was as sharp as the knitting needles in her skirt pocket. "Asking us to accept that questionable Kincaid fellow was one thing, but if you're going to start hauling in the street walkers—"

"Hold on, Myrtle," Joseph interrupted her. "You should be careful of your accusations. As for my intentions, when I accepted the call to the ministry— and it was a call, believe me!—I pledged mercy and love to all. No matter what a person has done, we're told in the Scripture to forgive. And to love. Now, that's part of my ministry, Myrtle. And I don't want

95

to offend you, but as long as I'm pastor of this church, I intend to extend help wherever it's needed."

"Then you may not be our pastor much longer!" she snapped, setting off across the grounds. "Come on, Elmer!" she yelled to her husband, who was happily sampling the apple cider. "We're leaving!" she ordered, her words seething with unspoken threats.

A dark red stain crept up the older man's thin face. Years of being overruled by Myrtle had whipped him into silent submission. Without a word, he turned and trudged after her, head down.

"Don't pay any attention to her." A young woman approached Kate and smiled. "Everyone has trouble with Myrtle! She can be very difficult at times, but the rest of us are very happy you came to our picnic."

For the first time, Kate smiled. "Do you really mean it? Well, then, I'm happy Jenny pestered me until I agreed to come." She glanced at Jenny, her green eyes glowing.

Soon the merriment of the afternoon had obliterated Myrtle's scene, and the afternoon passed in happy fellowship.

It was only after Jenny and Clint returned home that Clint's doubts surfaced. "Jenny, you did a very noble thing today. Taking Kate to the picnic, I mean."

"If you're happy about it, then why are you frowning?" Jenny studied his worried face.

"I'm afraid you're making trouble for yourself and particularly your father if you get too friendly with Kate. I hesitate to say this, but there is no guarantee that she will ever change her way of living."

Jenny's shoulders sagged wearily. The strain of the

day had taken its toll. And now the man whose support she had needed most appeared to question her judgment. "Clint, no one is asking for guarantees. Once Kate gets right with God, she won't want to go on living the way she has. She will change, Clint." Her violet eyes deepened with conviction. "I know she will."

Clint shoved his hands deep in the pockets of his gray trousers and strolled across the living room, staring thoughtfully at the clean fireplace, as though remembering the nights he recovered before that fire.

"Maybe she will. Maybe she won't. A person doesn't change as quickly and as easily as you seem to believe. You see, Jenny," he turned to face her, "you are a bit naïve when it comes to understanding human nature. You've lived a sheltered life in comparison to some people and—"

"Sheltered?" she cried. "Maybe I've been sheltered from some forms of sin, but I've met all types of people. What I'm not naive about, Clint, is the extent of God's forgiveness, and His ability to work miracles." She paced the room, staring blankly at the floor, reflecting on their conversation. "Clint, I don't know the mind of God, but it seems to me there are many types of sin. To me, vicious gossip is a form of murder—Myrtle Tubbs kills people with her sharp tongue. But whatever we've done, if we confess—"

"*Confess*?" Clint interrupted. "If a person confesses and is truly sorry, sure! But I haven't seen Kate making any confessions, have you?"

"How can you be so critical? I don't understand it, Clint. You, of all people, should be tolerant."

"Why me of all people?" he repeated, his lips twisted mockingly. "Ah, I see you haven't forgotten my past, after all! Is it because I haven't rushed up to the pulpit to make a Sunday morning confession?"

"I'm not referring to a public confession," she answered. "A person can make his peace with God privately." Her anger was slowly giving way to a growing hurt. "Clint, hasn't our faith in you made any difference?" she asked, her voice softened by the terrible ache in her throat. "We've believed in you. Everyone in the church believes in you, and yet, you want to persecute yourself—and me—by twisting my words. You know what I meant—that you should be tolerant of someone else's mistakes. You've admitted that you . . . have some problems," she swallowed.

"I just think you have a misconception about human nature," he snapped, pulling the angry blue eyes from her distraught face. "I'm sorry, but that's the way I feel. I've lived longer than you. I've seen more sin . . . and more pain."

"Have you?" she asked, her voice trembling. "You have a wonderful father, and, I am certain, a loving mother. You've been raised in ease and comfort." She tossed her dark head back and searched his lean face. "I never had a mother. And you don't know how much I've longed for one."

"Oh, Jenny, don't you think I know it hasn't been easy for you?" His eyes reflected his sympathy, yet his voice still carried a note of anger.

"The point is," she pressed further, "I don't know anything about the world you come from, Clint Kincaid! I only know that I'm glad I was not born into such a world if it leaves one too jaded for compassion!"

He glared at her, the full lips a tight line. The turquoise eyes were brilliant with restrained anger, but he merely turned and charged for the door.

"I think it's time to say goodbye." He opened the door and stormed out.

Jenny flew to the door and thrust it open. "I'm going to start holding a Bible class for the saloon girls, Clint Kincaid. What do you think of that?" she yelled.

Clint swung his long legs over the saddle, fitting his boots into the stirrups. 'I'd say that doesn't surprise me for a girl who's out to save the world!" He jabbed his heels into the horse's side, and the big stallion broke into a gallop.

"Not the world," she mumbled, tears spilling down her cheeks. "Just you and Kate."

True to her word, the next Wednesday afternoon Jenny sat in her living room, conducting a small Bible study. Only two people were present to hear her message, but this did not dampen Jenny's enthusiasm. Kate had actually come, bringing with her a woman named Belle, a maid at one of the hotels.

"Is that really true?" Belle demanded as Jenny finished reading a passage in Matthew. Belle's white head bobbed toward the Bible in Jenny's lap. Belle's troubles were heavily etched in the deep lines of her face. A lifetime of hard work had taken its toll on her thin, arthritic body, but her watery blue eyes were bright with hope.

"Is what true, Belle?" Jenny lifted questioning eyes.

"That there's a God who cares about us—even me," she added simply.

"I believe it, Belle," Jenny smiled. "I believe everything that was written in this Book."

The older woman sank back against the sofa, a new radiance illuminating her wrinkled face. "If only I had known that all these years. I had heard something 'bout it," she lifted her hands in a gesture of explanation, "but no one ever explained it to me the way you have."

"Jenny is a smart lady," Kate smiled. "I'm glad Belle and I came today. You've made me . . . happy, Jenny." Kate's green eyes were softened by her pleasant mood. "You've made me see that my life, even my future, isn't as hopeless as I thought."

"I'm so glad." Jenny looked from one woman to the other.

The sound of hoofbeats outside her door brought Jenny upright. She crossed to the window, her features suddenly tensing.

"Expecting someone?" Kate asked knowingly.

"Not really." Jenny dropped the curtain as the rider dismounted. One of the deacons was delivering a cake. A disappointed sigh escaped Jenny's lips.

She had tried to justify Clint's absence on Sunday by blaming the downpour of rain. But other doubts assailed her.

"Give him time." Kate tapped her shoulder. "He's crazy about you. Anyone can see that. It's just that Clint is a little preoccupied with this dream of gold— like so many others."

Jenny stared at her but said nothing. She was remembering their last conversation, the bitter argument that resulted in Clint's abrupt departure. She forced a weak smile.

"That's the way Clint is," Kate continued, a note of sympathy in her tone. "When he goes after something, it's all or nothing. Well, we'd better get back down the hill, right, Belle?"

Belle groaned. "I got floors to scrub. And just thinkin' about that makes my back hurt."

"Thank you for coming"—Jenny opened the door for them—"and try to bring more of your friends with you next week."

The man who stood on the doorstep was momentarily struck dumb by the sight of the hotel maid and the lady of the night emerging, happy smiles on their faces. He glanced over his shoulder as they waved goodbye, then he pushed a shy grin onto his wrinkled face.

"I got to hand it to you, Miss Jenny. You aren't bothered by profession or class."

"No, I'm not. Is that for us?"

"Yes'm. The missus was doing her weekly baking and she included an extra cake for you and the Reverend."

"How nice of her!"

"I was talking with your friend, Mr. Kincaid, this morning. He says the aspens are turning real pretty up in the high country."

Jenny's eyes widened in surprise. "You saw him in town this morning?"

"At the hardware store," he nodded. "He seems like a real nice fellow. Well, good day, Miss Jenny."

"Good day, Mr. Jackson. Oh, and remember to thank your wife for the cake," she called after him.

Jenny closed the door and stood with a puzzled frown crossing her face. So Clint was in Cripple Creek! Would he stop by, she wondered, or was he already on his way back to the mine?

Where's your faith? she chided herself, taking the cake to the kitchen. Of course he would stop by! He wouldn't let a silly little disagreement keep him away. And just to make a positive assertion of her faith, she put on a pot of coffee. He would have to pass near their street on his way back to the mining site. If she were going to teach faith in her Bible classes, she must practice more in her own life.

"Oh beautiful for spacious skies," she sang out, enjoying the popular new song by Katherine Bates, written after she stood on the summit of Pikes Peak.

Clint would come, she told herself, hurrying to her bedroom to freshen up. He simply must!

CHAPTER 8

JENNY STOOD BEFORE her living room window, drearily watching the rain etch sad little trails down the pane. Like angel tears, her father had told her as a child. She felt like shedding tears too, as she hugged her arms to herself in an effort to dispel the loneliness. It had rained throughout the week and into the weekend, and the brisk wind of September carried the threat of an early winter.

She sighed, moving away from the window.

What, she wondered, was going on in Clint's mind? He had not stopped by last week, nor had he come for Sunday services for the past two weeks. She could no longer make excuses for him. His feelings for her had obviously changed.

She sank down in the rocker and leaned her head against its frame. He had never told her he loved her. And even though Kate said he was "crazy about her," she had no assurance of that. Worse, it seemed, absence had increased her desire to see him, and now every hoofbeat on the road sent her hopes spiraling, only to be smashed again when days stretched on and Clint failed to appear.

She sighed, trying to think cheerful thoughts. Her Bible class this week, for instance. Kate and Belle had come again, bringing along two more women. The women were thin and undernourished, with a bleak hunger in their sad eyes. Jenny had not asked their professions, and no one had volunteered information.

Jenny recalled Kate's parting words and for a moment a surge of satisfaction brightened her mood.

"I've been thinking about going back to Denver," Kate had said. "Pray for me."

"I always do," Jenny had smiled. "I think going home would be good for you, Kate. Your family would be glad to have you back."

Kate had frowned. "I'm not sure. But Jenny," Kate had gripped her hand as tears flowed down her cheeks, "I don't want to go on living this way. I want to change."

Those words had brought a glow of happiness to Jenny, until now—until she thought of Clint.

"I seem to be able to help others, but I can't help myself!" she sighed. "I just can't get him out of my mind."

On Sunday morning, a rainbow arched the brilliant blue sky, and Jenny dressed for church with a prayer of thanksgiving. At last the weather had improved.

To her surprise, a familiar, fawn stallion was tied to the hitching rail before the store when she arrived for church. At the sight of Clint's horse, her steps faltered on the board sidewalk. She felt eager, yet nervous, about seeing him again. *Stop this*, she scolded herself.

I can't let him turn my world upside down again. I can't!

But as she hurried through the store and entered the meeting area, her nervousness increased. Scanning the crowd she spotted Clint right away, chatting amicably with the man who had delivered the cake. He was dressed in a new black suit that accentuated the golden sheen of his hair. As though sensing her arrival, he turned, and curious blue eyes searched her out.

She blinked, forced a tentative smile, then moved on. As she made her way up the aisle to the choir chairs, she tried to analyze her feelings. She was annoyed and, yes, hurt that he had avoided her. But if she were going to be the loving example she wanted to be, wouldn't it be silly to pout? *Silly, but human*, she thought honestly.

"Hello, Jenny." Catching up with her, he reached for her hand.

She lifted questioning violet eyes to the piercing blue ones, and then, for one breathless moment she forgot that they were blocking the church aisle, forgot everything, as they stood staring at one another.

"Hello," she murmured. Then someone nudged her, and she realized it was time for the music to begin. "Excuse me," she said and hurried to her chair.

For the first time, Jenny heard nothing her father said. She stared at her open Bible, trying to follow his text, but every fiber of her being was atuned to the man in the back row. And she wondered if he, too, were really listening to the sermon.

She decided not to glance toward Clint again, for each time she had, his blue eyes pinned hers, and she sat mesmerized until, with great effort, she forced her gaze away.

Self-conscious, she stared down at her new dress. Slim fingers traced the luxurious softness of the dark silk. Her cousin Rebecca had sent the dress to her from St. Louis. Rebecca was an inch shorter and a few pounds heavier but Jenny had found it a simple matter to lengthen the garment and take in the sides to fit her own slender figure. The only quality dresses in her closet had come from Rebecca, who quickly tired of her excessive wardrobe, and packed an occasional dress off to Jenny, whom she considered to be living in uncivilized territory. And true, her plain skirts, blouses, and dresses seemed so out of date compared to a dress like this one. Jenny shifted her position on the hard bench, and the silk rustled.

She felt a gentle nudge. "The invitation hymn," the woman next to her whispered.

Jenny blinked in surprise, glancing wide-eyed at the crowd who sat waiting for the music to begin. How had she allowed her thoughts to wander? Jenny cleared her throat, flipping through the pages.

She lifted her head and sang in a clear sweet voice, trying not to see the blazing blue eyes that never left hers, nor to hear the rich, baritone voice that filled the rear of the building. It was so good to have him back. How could she possibly be angry with him?

A smile touched her lips, and the room seemed to glow with her happiness. Even the congregation seemed especially joyous this morning.

As the service ended, the woman beside her turned to ask a question. From the corner of her eye, she could see Clint approaching.

Jenny stammered an appropriate reply to the woman, then turned to gather up the hymnals. Suddenly, Clint was standing beside her, waiting for her to acknowledge his presence.

She straightened, adjusting the small black toque on her upswept curls. "Hello, Clint." She looked at him with a welcoming smile. "How have you been?"

"Very well." His eyes swept over her, then glowed with approval. "And I can see for myself that you are well."

"Thank you," she responded, trying to match his pleasant mood.

"I know I haven't given you any advance notice, but I was wondering if you could spend the afternoon with me. I have something I want to show you."

Her dark brows arched inquiringly as she tried to remember her plans for the day. The Burtons! They were coming for Sunday dinner, and then she had promised to play checkers with their young son.

"I'm so sorry," she sighed. "We've invited a new family to share lunch with us. Maybe . . . ," she hesitated, realizing there was scarcely enough to feed the Burtons, not to mention Clint.

"That's all right." He made an effort to conceal his disappointment. "I should have asked sooner. What about tomorrow?"

"Tomorrow?" she echoed, wondering what he had in mind.

"The aspens are turning in the mountains, and the view might be worth the trip."

"Oh?" She was pleasantly surprised. "Well, that sounds nice. Tell me, has your mine started to produce yet?"

"Not yet. But we're digging deeper each day. This week I found some interesting-looking ore embedded

107

in a crack of solid rock. I've ordered more dynamite and now we're just waiting for the right supplies in order to cut through that rock."

"Well, good luck," Jenny smiled.

"That's a pretty dress you're wearing," His eyes swept over her again.

"Thank you." At his kindness, the old tenderness surfaced in her heart, along with the dull ache of rejection. Why had he stayed away? She bit her lip, fearful she might suddenly ask him that question. Unless he chose to explain, she would be remiss in asking. He was here now. That was all that really mattered.

"Well, I'll catch up on my rest at the hotel today," he said, glancing around them and noticing most of the crowd had left. "May I come for you early in the morning?"

"Of course. Shall I pack a picnic basket?"

"No," he grinned. "I'll ask the hotel dining room to prepare lunch for us. I'm looking forward to our day together," he added softly.

"So am I." The sadness that had filled her eyes for days suddenly vanished. Now Jenny was as radiant as the sparkling rainbow beyond the church window.

Aspen leaves, like gold coins, drifted onto the rutted path as Clint guided the horses up the narrow trail. Jenny sat on the wagon seat, drinking in the splendor of the aspen groves surrounding them.

"Oh, Clint! It's beautiful here." She turned back to him, her eyes glowing with child-like wonder. "I'm so glad we came."

The lavender shawl draped over Jenny's shoulders was a perfect foil for her blue-purple eyes. They seemed to reflect the mellow light of an autumn day. Her dark hair swung about her face, which was stung by the wind to a rosy hue.

Her generous lips spread in a warm smile as she met Clint's glance.

"How much farther?" she asked.

"Just over the next hill."

The road dipped through another meadow where the grass rippled like gold silk beneath the sweeping wind. Autumn wildflowers provided a rainbow of lime, dusty rose, and soft plum. The surrounding beauty brought another appreciative sigh from Jenny.

"It's so peaceful here. I can see why you never come to town."

His golden brows arched skeptically. "It isn't the scenery that keeps me in these mountains. It's the work. Well, here we are." He leaned back on the reins to halt the horses, and their heads dipped to sample the sweet lush grass.

"This is the Nellie B," Clint announced proudly, pointing to the deep shaft before them. "Named after my mother, Nell Bransford Kincaid. All mining claims must have a name, you know." He glanced back at her, a mischievous grin lighting his eyes. "If I had known you at the time I staked my claim, I would have christened it the Jenny T!"

Jenny burst into laughter. "I think Nellie B sounds much better. Anyway, I think it's very sweet of you to name your mining claim after your mother."

"Mother has always supported my ideas, no matter how radical they might have appeared to others." He crossed to her side of the wagon to help her down. "Even though my father wanted me to be an executive in the lumber business, my mother understood my dreams and encouraged me."

I'd like to know her," Jenny said, watching him thoughtfully.

"And she'd like to know you. Perhaps she and my father will come down for Christmas."

"Wonderful! I shall invite them for Sunday dinner and . . . ." She hesitated as she considered the contrast her humble home would present to the wealthy woman. "Our cabin will seem like a matchbox to your mother, I imagine." Her smile faded.

Clint reached for her hand. "She will be more interested in you than in where you live. Come on, let's walk over to the shaft."

Jenny's fingers curled around his strong ones, and she felt her heart quicken as they walked. It was wonderful being here with him, sharing the thing that was the most important to him. She lifted her eyes to scan the surrounding foothills, scarred with prospect holes and an occasional shaft.

"How did you happen to choose this spot?" she glanced around the quiet meadow.

"I talked to an old prospector in town. He said some ore samples from this valley were rich in gold. I spoke with some people in the assayer's office and found that to be true. So I staked my claim and started digging."

"Do prospectors still pan for gold?" she asked curiously, thinking that seemed easier than seeking gold buried deep in the earth.

"Some still pan the streams," Clint answered, "and occasionally someone gets lucky. But panning was more successful around Denver in the late fifties and early sixties. Here, we have to go deep in the earth—but when I strike my El Dorado, it will be worth the trouble."

110

Jenny nodded, staring down into the deep hole before them.

Vertical planks supported the black-loam dirt, presenting a barrier against the crumbling walls of earth. A shiver raced over Jenny as she imagined Clint spending his days underground where there was always the danger of a cave-in.

"A tunnel leads back from the shaft," Clint pointed. "We're testing a wall of rock in the tunnel. Say a prayer for my good fortune." He lifted a hand to tap her cheek affectionately.

"And your safety," she added worriedly.

Clint gave a fearless laugh.

"Well, that's about all I can show you from this angle. If you'd care to climb down the shaft for a closer look, you could examine some interesting-looking ore."

"No thanks!" Jenny automatically stepped back. "While I'm quite fascinated with the Nellie B, I think I prefer to hear about the mine, rather than investigate it closely. The Nellie B . . . ?" A mischievous glint lit her eyes. "I've often wondered about this lady who requires so much of your time."

"I have been working hard," he acknowledged with a sigh, "and I must work even harder. The old-timers are predicting an early winter. There's a lot to be done before the weather sets in."

As they reached the wagon, Jenny found that her appetite had been sharpened by the walk and by the fresh air.

"Let me help," she said, reaching for the white linen cloth covering the basket. Her hand brushed his, and a look of tenderness filled Clint's eyes as he set the basket down, then gently removed the tablecloth from her arms.

His hand cupped her chin, tilting her head back so he could look deeply into her eyes. "You add a very special beauty to this mountainside," he said, as he lowered his lips to hers. The touch of his lips sent Jenny's arms up his broad shoulders. For one breathless moment, she forgot everything in the joy of that kiss. Then suddenly Clint released her and stepped back, seemingly distracted by an eagle circling the sky.

"Clint, what's wrong?" Jenny asked shyly, wishing she could read his mind.

"Nothing." When he turned back to her, she sensed a reserve about him and wondered why. "Shall we have lunch?" he asked, an edge to his voice as he lifted the picnic basket again.

He was exploring the contents of the basket, pulling out containers of food. Jenny turned to spread the cloth over a smooth patch of ground.

"This looks more like a gourmet feast than a picnic lunch," she said with a smile.

"Well, we'll see if the dining room prepares a picnic basket as well as they prepare their dinners."

The two sat down to the food and Jenny offered grace. After the tasty meal, Clint stood up and stretched, then glanced back at Jenny.

"Let's go for a walk," he suggested.

His relaxed smile brought a sigh of relief to Jenny. She had scarcely enjoyed the delicious food. Even though there had been periods of companionable silence on their ride up, those same lengthy silences now seemed to separate them.

"A walk sounds wonderful," Jenny replied, grateful for the exercise. "Why don't we gather up the remains of the picnic and load the wagon first?"

112

Clint glanced at the mess. "It takes a woman to create order." He leaned down to help her. "When I'm with you, I'm aware of all the things I miss living by myself here on this mountainside."

Jenny continued folding the cloth. "Well, I suppose men aren't inclined to think of dirty dishes and housework."

"Oh, it isn't the dirty dishes," he sighed. "It's the loneliness when the cold wind howls around my little shack, or when I get up in the morning and see a glorious new sunrise and there's no one to share it."

Jenny stared at him, reflecting on those words. She, too, had known that kind of aching void when feelings needed to be shared. Good or bad. Of course she had her father. Still . . . She closed her mind to further thoughts.

"There," she said, brushing her hands together as Clint replaced the basket in the wagon. "Shall we take that walk now?"

"Yep." Clint slipped his arm around her shoulder as they began to stroll across the grounds. "This day has been about perfect as far as I can tell."

He fell silent again, staring at the mine shaft ahead of them. "I think you're about perfect, except for your belief that everyone is as idealistic as you."

"Please, Clint," she frowned, pushing a dark strand of hair from her face. "Let's not argue." There was a quiet plea in her voice.

"We won't," he said. "And after your telling me about those Bible classes, and Kate's new attitude, I guess it's a good thing you do believe the best about people."

She tossed her thick hair back from her face and studied the deep cavity in the earth, the glory hole that Clint hoped would make him rich.

"I do hope you strike," she glanced at Clint, "if that's what you really want."

"Of course it's what I want!" He stared down at her, the turquoise eyes incredulous. "I keep forgetting that you place so little importance on money." He shook his head in dismay.

"Maybe because we never had it," Jenny shrugged. "You can't miss what you've never had."

"It isn't the money," he said quietly, "it's . . . proving something. And I must . . ."

"Really, Clint? What must you prove?"

"That I can do it! I have to stand on my own, don't you see? I have to accomplish something as Clint Kincaid. Not as Calvin Kincaid's son or . . . ." He broke off, staring thoughtfully at the mine. "It's down there," his voice was tense. "I know the gold is there." His arm tightened around her shoulder. "Have you heard the story of the man who came up in these hills, dug around a little, then gave it up? Someone else bought his claim and dug another two feet. Guess what he found?"

"Gold," Jenny replied, having heard the story many times. It was the inspiration miners fed one another when poverty and hunger threatened.

"Gold in the millions!"

"But—"

"But what if I bankrupt myself and my father and find nothing?" He heaved a deep sigh, his broad shoulders straining against his plaid flannel shirt. "I guess I will just have to gamble that the Nellie B is going to pay off. Not gamble," he corrected, grinning. "I don't gamble anymore. I only went to the blackjack table a couple of times out of curiosity."

"I believe that you're a good man, Clint—no matter how you try to insist that you're not."

"Not good, but better, Jenny," he said, staring at a speck on the next hill.

Jenny turned to study his face. Following his gaze to the distant hills, she noticed a tiny cabin where someone had once lived. Probably a miner. Then, as they stood looking at the landscape, a figure ran from the woods toward the cabin.

She glanced at Clint as he took a step forward, squinting into the sun. Then suddenly she remembered the man who had been his neighbor.

"Clint," she swallowed, "is that cabin away over there where—where Benson lived?"

He nodded, continuing to assess the distant cabin through slitted lids.

"I thought I smelled woodsmoke a few minutes ago," he said. "Now I see a man sneaking around the side of that cabin."

"Is it . . . *Benson*?" The mention of that name brought a knot of fear to her throat.

"I don't know." He turned to her. "Don't look. Whoever it is, he's watching us. Just keep talking while we walk back to the wagon." He slipped his arm around her shoulder, but this time the pressure of his fingers almost brought a cry of pain to her lips.

"Clint," she swallowed. "Let's just get in the wagon and go after the Sheriff. That's the most sensible thing to do." The suggestion was prompted by an intuitive feeling that Clint was about to do something rash.

"There isn't time. We're going to walk back to the wagon. Then I'm going to get a horse and ride over there."

"No, Clint!" she whirled, grabbing his arm. "If it is Benson, he's a dangerous man. He's already hurt you."

"But he isn't going to hurt me again! In a fair fight I can beat him. The only reason I got hurt before was because I turned my back.

"No, Clint!" she cried, unable to resist searching the distance for any sign of the man.

"Jenny! Stop staring!" he commanded, and in spite of himself, he threw one last glance at the cabin on the next hill. Then he whirled back to the horses, quickly unhitching one.

The horse free, Clint ran to the back of the wagon, and pulled out a shotgun. Then he leaped on the horse.

"Stay here!" he yelled to her, as he spurred the horse's flanks and galloped off.

"Clint!" she screamed. "Don't go! Please!"

She ran after him, then stopped, panting. How foolish to think she could stop him. There was no stopping Clint Kincaid once he made up his mind to do something.

"God, help him," she moaned, as horse and rider raced down the hill and across the valley.

CHAPTER 9

FOR ONE BREATHLESS MOMENT. Jenny felt a strong impulse to unhitch a horse and ride after Clint. But Clint would be furious with her, she decided, leaning against the rough wood of the wagon in an effort to still her trembling body.

She buried her face in her hands, wondering what to do. Clint had a gun. What if he killed Benson?

"Oh, no," she moaned, jerking her hands down from her stricken face and running to the vantage point where they had stood. She could not see Clint! She caught her breath as her eyes scanned the woods behind the cabin. Then, squinting into the sunlight, she glimpsed a dim movement through the woods. The longer she watched, the more she was certain it was Clint.

She clenched her hands together, every muscle in her body stiff with fear as she watched him carefully approach the back of the cabin.

Her eyes swung over to the tiny hut. Was Benson

inside, waiting to shoot Clint if he tried to sneak up to the door?

"Hardheaded cuss, ain't he? He shoulda learned to steer clear of me!"

The rough voice that she had hoped never to hear again struck her like a blow. Her blood froze in her veins as she turned slowly to face Benson.

He swaggered toward her with an air of crude confidence. Far in the distance his slab-ribbed buckskin was tethered to a sturdy pine. How had he managed to creep up on her, she thought, frantic.

She swallowed, lifting her chin in an effort to conceal her fear. She must not anger him, yet she would not allow herself to shrink beneath the bloodshot stare.

He seemed taller than ever—though perhaps a few pounds thinner. The shaggy red beard and tobacco-stained teeth made him even more repulsive than before.

"You had already seen us, hadn't you?" Jenny asked, stalling for time as her mind spun with possibilities for escape.

"Yep. Been waitin' for him to come back. Figgered on catching him at night while he was asleep. But then when you showed up with him . . . "—a vulgar laugh broke the stillness—"I knew I'd struck it rich!"

"Why would you want to harm him again?" Jenny tossed her dark head back to glare into the ugly, red-bearded face. "Haven't you done enough? And why do you want me?" Her cheeks colored as soon as the question was spoken and she dropped her head, silently begging God for help.

"I ain't got enough money to git as far as I need to go. Now Mr. Kincaid, he's got plenty of money. And I figger he'll pay a nice little sum to get you back."

"What are you going to do?" Jenny asked.

"You and me is gonna take a little ride. And I'm dependin' on you to be real quiet."

"I'm not going anywhere with you," she replied, trying to still the tremor in her voice.

"You'll go. Or I'll kill you now, then waylay your boyfriend."

Jenny felt as though her knees would buckle as he pulled a length of rope from his pocket and jerked her hands behind her.

"Let me go!" she cried. "I'll scream, I'll . . ."

With one large hand easily restraining her arms behind her, he yanked a knife from its scabbard and flashed it recklessly before her face.

Jenny swallowed, staring in terror at the long blade, its sharp metal glinting in the bright sunlight. A warm dizziness clouded her vision. She couldn't faint; she couldn't.

At her silence, he returned the knife to the scabbard and concentrated on binding her wrists. The rope cut into her delicate skin, but Jenny bit her lip, forcing back a cry of pain.

"Come on," he growled, shoving her ahead of him. She stumbled up the path, feeling awkward and off-balance with her hands behind her. He marched her to Clint's cabin and kicked the narrow door open.

Jenny stared into the dimness of the cluttered one-room hut, feeling a sudden ache in her heart as her eyes lingered on Clint's belongings, stacked neatly beside his bedroll on the dirt floor. At the far end of the room, a crude little table held tin cups and plates and a few eating utensils.

Benson lumbered about, searching. Before her mind could devise a plan, Jenny's eyes scanned the eating area, not yet aware what she was seeking, yet knowing she needed something to defend herself.

Her breath caught in her throat as her search ended with a pocket-knife left beside a small washpan on a low board nailed to the wall. Her feet moved silently in that direction.

Benson was bent over the bedroll, tossing Clint's clothing in a careless heap. Jenny stationed herself in front of the board, being sure her body concealed the weapon. Slowly, she bent her knees so that her bound hands could retrieve the knife.

A split second before Benson cast a suspicious glance in her direction, Jenny straightened.

Apparently satisfied that she was not trying to escape, Benson returned to his plundering, finally retrieving writing paper and pen. He grunted uncomfortably as he leaned down to scrawl something on the paper.

This is it! Jenny thought with a flash of panic. If she had any hopes of getting the knife, it had to be this second. Counting on his preoccupation with the note, she glanced back over her shoulder, locating the exact spot on the board where the knife rested. Then she bent her knees again, and her fingers crept along the board, seeking and finding the knife. It felt cold and clumsy in her palm.

What now? she thought, staring at Benson. There was no way she could keep it concealed in her hand. If she could twist her upper body enough to allow her hands to extend to her left skirt pocket . . . .

The pen made scratching sounds on the paper as Benson labored over the message. Jenny seized the final seconds to twist her torso sharply so that her hands could reach her side pocket.

Pain shot through her side at the wrenching of her body, but the knife slipped down into the depths of her pocket.

"Come on!" he yelled, tossing the pen down. "And be quick about it!" The beady eyes shot a warning. "He's probably figgered out by now that I ain't at the cabin."

Silently she obeyed, trying to walk quickly, but not being quick enough to please the sullen Benson. His fingers bit through the sleeves of her blouse as he seized her arm and dragged her roughly out of the cabin toward his horse.

She was forced to run in order to match his long steps. "Get on," he rasped, busily untying his horse.

Jenny lifted her foot to the stirrup but without the use of her hands, her movements were clumsy. With a snort of impatience, Benson hauled her up into the saddle. She risked a frightened glance toward the patch of woods that separated her from Clint. There was nothing she could do now—she was at the mercy of a man who appeared to have no mercy. Only God could save her from Benson who was capable of anything, even murder . . . regardless of whether Clint gave him the ransom money or not.

Benson was climbing on behind her, and she could feel the poor horse sag beneath its cruel load. His nearness, as he reached around her to rein the horse, brought a rancid smell of tobacco and whiskey. It was almost like a physical assault.

His spurs jabbed the mount's flanks, and they galloped heedlessly into the deep woods north of the cabin. At first Jenny was bounced about as helpless as a rag doll. Without the use of her hands on the saddle horn, she felt she would topple any minute. The only way she could maintain her balance was to lean forward in the saddle, putting strain on her back.

Just staying in the saddle as they galloped through the dense woods required her utmost concentration, yet some deeper logic took over, forcing her to note the direction they were taking.

Benson had struck a trail through unfamiliar woods that deepened and became a blur in their reckless speed. A low-hanging branch scraped her face, and the wind pounded in her ears. Benson spurred the horse on as if Clint were already in pursuit. If only he were! But Jenny was certain he was still exploring the distant foothills they had left behind, diligently seeking the cruel man who had just added kidnapping to his list of crimes.

Jenny had no idea how many miles they had covered. She only knew they were traveling north. Every bone in her body ached in protest. She had no choice but to suffer in silence.

Then suddenly the horse broke into a clearing, and a narrow stream meandered through a valley of cottonwoods. Mount Ryalite lay to their left, its rugged beauty bringing a sigh of relief to Jenny's dry lips. She still had a vague sense of where they were.

Benson urged the horse into the stream and yanked it to a halt. The horse quickly dipped his head to quench his thirst and Jenny lurched forward. Just before she plunged over the horse's neck, a hammy hand shot out and grabbed her shoulders. He tightened the reins again and the horse clomped awkwardly over the rocky bed as they followed the crooked trail of the stream. The icy water splashed onto Jenny's feet, dampening the hem of her skirt.

What would happen to her? And to Clint? How

could she hope to escape from this brute of a man, she thought with rising fear.

Nothing is impossible with God, she told herself. Maybe Clint would come after her; maybe he was already racing back to Cripple Creek for the Sheriff. She had to keep her spirits up. She remembered the knife in her pocket, and her heart beat faster. She would use it to cut the rope—if they ever stopped riding and if she could escape Benson's watchful glare. *So many if's,*she thought, her hopes plummeting again.

She would find a way, she argued stubbornly, aware that she must not give over to panic or depression, both thieves of common sense. She swallowed against the awful dryness of her mouth, as Benson urged the horse out of the stream and up yet another hill.

Quickly she scanned the woods, watching the slant of the afternoon sun through the pines and aspens. Everything looked the same to her. When she tried to glance down at the trail, overlaid with pine needles and aspen leaves, she felt herself sliding from the saddle.

"Sit still!" he roared in her ear. Wearily, she straightened, pushing her aching back into the forward position again.

She continued to stare at the dense woods until suddenly a ray of hope lit her path, like the sunlight filtering through the treetops.

Just ahead, a tall pine half obscured the trail, an ugly twisted pine whose long trunk bore the slim scar of lightning. She had seen that kind of scar on another pine near their home. Her father had explained that lightning often struck timber at this high altitude.

They climbed two more hills before approaching a

small deserted camp in the shelter of a pine thicket. Benson sawed the reins against the horse's foaming mouth, jerking them to a halt. He slid off the horse and lumbered toward the camp, glancing right and left as though making sure they were alone.

Jenny quickly followed his searching glance, noting the bed of ashes surrounding the small circle of rocks and the distant canvas stretched over two pine saplings. Apparently, this was where he had been hiding out.

"Get off the horse," he commanded as he continued to survey the quiet woods surrounding them.

Jenny tried to dismount carefully, but without the use of her hands, she ended up plunging headlong into the dirt. In the fall she managed to shift her weight to her left side, fearing the knife might slip from her pocket.

Benson looked across at her in disgust then turned to hobble his horse. With his back turned, Jenny cast a quick glance toward her pocket, noting with joy the small bulge there. It was a miracle that she had not lost the knife over the bumpy terrain or now in this awkward plunge to the ground.

Slowly, she pulled herself up and limped to a distant aspen. Her ankle had begun to throb, but she scarcely noticed. She was numb with fatigue and shock, and her throat was as dry as the dust on her skirt. She forced herself to think, to seek a level place where she could place her back against the trunk of a tree.

Benson was plundering through his saddlebag and she realized this was the best opportunity for sneaking the knife from her pocket. Her eyes dropped to her skirt, realizing there was an easier way to withdraw the knife than painfully twisting her torso. She gripped the waistband of her skirt and tugged it around so that her left pocket was directly behind her.

If she could get the knife from her pocket, then drop down against the tree, she might eventually saw through the rope while Benson was not watching.

Benson was hauling things out of his saddlebag and Jenny took a deep breath, gathering her courage before stretching her fingers down into her pocket to seek the knife. As her fingers closed over it, Benson darted a scowling glance over his shoulder.

Fear shivered through her, buckling her knees. This time she obeyed her weak body, dropping to the ground to lean back against the aspen. In her trembling hand the knife held fast.

She blinked across at Benson, noting that his large hands cradled a canteen, a strip of dried jerky, and— her heart raced—a bottle of whiskey.

Perspiration dotted her forehead, dampening the loose tendrils of hair that had sprung. How could she get the knife open without cutting herself? She sat rigid, her heart racing, her breath labored.

"You hungry?" he yelled.

She jumped, unable to quiet her taut nerves.

"No." Her voice held the raspy note of panic.

"Too good to eat my jerky?" he sneered, lumbering over to the bed of ashes.

"No, I'm just not hungry," she replied. It would be her undoing to anger him now.

Her eyes fell on a battered coffeepot near the ashes. "If you're going to build a fire, I would like some coffee," she added shyly.

That would divert him for a few minutes, she thought, gripping the knife tighter.

"A fancy miss like you don't drink my kind of

coffee," he eyed her suspiciously. "Besides, I ain't interested in coffee. I need somethin' a lot stronger."

Jenny's eyes widened as he uncorked his whiskey bottle.

Her eyes few back to the canteen beside his saddlebag. She craved a drink of water, but wondered if she could force herself to drink from his canteen.

"You can have some water," he heaved a sigh, following her gaze.

When she did not reply, he yanked up the canteen and strode over to her, impatiently removing the lid.

She could feel his hot brooding stare as her eyes lingered on the extended canteen.

"I don't want to drink all of your water," she mumbled, hoping he would find a stream and get more, thus giving her an opportunity to work on the rope.

"Still trying to be the goody-goody, are you? Here! Drink! We got a few hours to wait and I ain't in the mood for any whinin'."

He pressed the canteen to her parched lips and the water trickled into her dry mouth. Strange that a few sips of water could provide instant relief, she thought, but she felt new strength surge through her as he stepped back, recapping the canteen.

"What are we waiting here for?" she asked, remembering his words.

"For your boyfriend to get his money together. That little message I left oughta have him ridin' break-neck to the banker by now."

"He may be riding break-neck for the Sheriff."

"Maybe," Benson shrugged, ambling back over to his whiskey. "But I reckon he values your life more'n that."

Jenny swallowed, studying the evil man before her. "Are you swapping me for the money?" she asked.

"Don't get too nosy," he barked. "You just sit there and keep quiet."

Jenny bit her lip, glancing up at the sky. An hour until dark, she estimated, hoping to keep her wits until the whiskey mellowed him, or made him careless.

She had to do it now, she told herself, dreading the moment she must open the knife. She had no idea how long it would take to saw through the rope, but while he was occupied with his whiskey, he was less likely to notice her movements.

What if she accidentally slit her wrist? It was quite likely that Benson would do nothing to prevent her from bleeding to death. Could she pry the blade out and saw the rope in half without cutting herself?

I can do all things through Christ who strengthens me. She repeated the verse in her mind as her fingers worked with the blade of the knife. With her eyes fixed on an aspen leaf dancing on a light breeze, she slowly opened the knife and positioned the sharp blade against the strip of rope. She could feel more drops of perspiration gathering on her brow.

Was this the right thing to do? Would she be smarter to take her chances with Benson? She caught his evil stare on her again and decided not.

"Are you really from St. Louis?" she asked, knowing she needed conversation to calm herself.

He grunted. 'There—and a few other places."

"And you need the money to get back to St. Louis?" she asked, slowly beginning to saw the rope.

"I need the money to keep runnin'." He was staring morosely at the bottle in his hand. "I been on the run for years. It's why I'm in Colorado. Got

127

accused for a murder I didn't commit back East. Nobody would believe me. Now it don't matter."

Jenny stared at him, trying to absorb his words, as her fingers worked the knife. "But you can't keep on running for the rest of your life." Then she remembered what he had done to Clint. "Unless you keep committing crimes. You did try to kill Clint, didn't you? You can't blame that on someone else."

He sat glaring at the bottle for a long moment; then he turned sullen eyes on her again. "I wasn't gonna shoot him. I just needed his money. Then he turned around and saw I was about to hit him over the head. I—I didn't have no choice."

Jenny stopped sawing momentarily. "But you do have a choice as to what you'll do with me. And with the ransom money you're getting from Clint. You don't have to do this, you know. You could let me go and then I would find Clint and tell him—"

He gave a hoarse ugly laugh. "You're kinda stupid, Miss Jenny Townley. Why would I go to all this trouble just to turn you loose and then have that headstrong Kincaid on my trail? I know what I'm doin'." His eyes narrowed to thin slits in his red-bearded face. "And I ain't gonna change my mind. It's too late," he growled, tilting the bottle again.

"It's never too late," she countered, forgetting her resolve not to anger him. "Don't you see you're going to be running for the rest of your life? And what kind of life is that?"

"The only one I got!" he snarled, swiping the sleeve of his flannel shirt across his mouth. "There ain't . . . nothin' else . . . now."

His words were beginning to slur, and Jenny saw that the bottle was half empty. Was he one of those men who couldn't stop drinking once he started? Her father had spoken of such men. An unexpected sadness filled her as she studied the big man. There was a bleakness in his eyes, his words, a terrible despair that hid beneath his anger and meanness.

"Mr. Benson, you don't want to go on like this for the rest of your life," she pleaded softly. "Have you ever thought about asking God to forgive you?"

"Shut up!" he yelled. "I don't want to hear no preachin'. Leave that to your pa!" An evil glare hardened his gaze. "You better be real nice to me—I could make you sorry if you ain't."

Jenny swallowed, forcing herself to speak bravely. "Listen to me, Mr. Benson. I may not be as strong as you, but I have a God who is. I don't think you want to harm me." She hesitated, waiting to measure the effect of her words on him. He slumped back, staring at her. "If you remember, Father and I showed you kindness and respect. That's the least you can do for me now," she added.

Slowly, the anger faded from his face as the evil look dulled to a glassy stare. He merely grunted and reached for his bottle.

Jenny pressed the knife harder against the rope. She felt the sharp prick of the blade on her skin and knew she would start bleeding. If the wound was deep, there was no way she could conceal the blood from Benson. In the midst of her frenzied thoughts, she heard the soft snap of the rope and felt the bindings break free.

Arching her back, she twisted her neck to venture a glance over her shoulder. Joy mingled with concern as she saw that her hands were free, yet there was a large smear of blood on her left arm. She dropped the knife and straightened, vowing to deal with one problem at a time. She flexed her fingers to restore circulation as she glanced across at Benson.

His head had begun to slump on his barrel-like chest. Hope surged through her at the possibility of escape. Garbled snores filled the air, and she withdrew her hands from her back, quickly assessing the damage to her arm. There was a steady flow of blood from a shallow cut, one that would require bandaging as soon as she was safely away. She breathed a sigh of relief at the realization that she had not slashed a vein.

Slowly she crept to her feet, careful not to step on a twig or rustle her skirts. With her eyes set determinedly on the path to the horse, she tiptoed around Benson, her bleeding arm wrapped in a corner of her skirt.

In the back of her mind, she perceived the danger of his waking suddenly, and she was torn between immediate, careless flight or slow, cautious escape. She chose caution—first rubbing the horse's damp neck, then leaning down to unhobble him. Drops of blood stained golden aspen leaves at her feet as she worked with the horse. She would not bleed to death, she told herself, trying to quiet her mounting panic at the sight of her blood. When the horse was free, she leaped up on its back and dug her heels into its side. As they plunged through the dense woods, she could hear Benson's shouts, threats, and curses, but she leaned into the wind, her fingers gripping the saddle horn. The horse seemed almost as eager as Jenny to be free of Benson.

The sun had set, and as darkness closed over her, all the pines began to look the same. Even the aspens, now a softened blur of molten gold, gave her no sense of direction. The horse plunged on, obviously having no problem with direction. Jenny could only pray they were taking the same trail that led to the stream.

When she glanced at her arm, she saw the blood had soaked through the makeshift bandage.

Then the woods thinned before her and a tall, deformed tree jutted into her path, silhouetted awkwardly against the rising moon. It was the scarred tree, beautiful beyond belief in its grotesque uniqueness. There was no other like it. She was on the right trail.

Relief swept over her and she yanked the reins, slowing the horse to a trot. Her breath came in gulps, her hair hung in her face, and she was cold to the bone, now that the lingering warmth of the sun had disappeared. Silently, she prayed.

Ahead, through the dark pines, the silver glint of the stream reflected the first light of the moon. The stream was like a beacon to her, drawing her over the shadowed trail. At the sight of water, the horse galloped toward the winding stream and lurched to a halt at the edge. Jenny loosened the reins and gripped the saddle horn, steadying herself as the horse dipped his head to drink.

Through the darkness, another horse nickered softly and Jenny's heart leaped to her throat. Her eyes widened with fear as she glanced left to right, seeing far down the stream, the silhouette of horse and rider. She froze, her blood pounding through her veins. Did she dare call to the dark form, or would she merely be inviting danger of a different kind?

Scarcely moving, she watched the horse loping slowly toward her. Her teeth sank into her bottom lip as she sat frozen between fear and hope. Then as the tan stallion drew closer and the broad-shouldered man became a familiar form, she cried out in disbelief.

"Clint! Clint, is that you?"

"Jenny!"

He leapt from the horse and ran toward her. In the moonlight, his lean face was drawn with worry, yet the blue eyes glowed with joy as he reached up for her.

When he pulled her down into his arms, his joy faded.

"Jenny! You're hurt! What happened?"

"I accidentally cut my arm with your knife . . . the one I sneaked from your cabin when Benson left the note."

He stared in disbelief. Clearly, he did not understand the explanation, but he wasted no time with questions. He whirled back to his saddlebag, pulling out a clean bandana. "I'll bind it tightly to stop the flow." He frowned. "Then we'll get to a doctor. Jenny," the square jaw clenched, "did he hurt you in any way?"

"No. He bound my wrists to keep me from running away. Then when we got to his camp, he started drinking and dozed off for a minute. I cut the rope and grabbed his horse . . . ." She was beginning to feel dizzy and she leaned against him gratefully.

"Thank God!" He tied the corners of the bandage into a hard knot then wrapped his arms around her. "I tore out like a madman when I came back and found the note. I was able to follow his tracks to the stream, but I lost him here," a heavy sigh wrenched his body.

"Yes," she remembered. "We went downstream for maybe a quarter of a mile." She leaned back to look up into his taut face. "He's camped a few miles up in the woods. Do you . . . still want to find him?"

"No. Catching Benson isn't worth endangering your life again. I've learned my lesson—the hard way, of course. We're heading for the doctor right now. Then later the Sheriff and I will deal with Benson. I should never have left you, Jenny. Can you forgive me?"

"Of course I can. You had no way of knowing what he would do."

"I should never have left you," he repeated, his voice husky as his head dipped and his lips brushed hers. "I'll make it up to you, I promise."

She tried to smile but his face was blurring before her. She leaned against his chest, taking deep gulps of the chill night air to clear her head. His strong arms cradled her shoulders, lifting her easily into the saddle.

"Clint, I'm so glad you found me," she whispered, feeling her strength ebb away.

He sighed, shaking his dark head. "You found me, Jenny. You're a very courageous woman."

He lingered only a second, his eyes filled with tenderness before he turned back for his horse. Quietly they made their way home to Cripple Creek.

CHAPTER 10

MAUDE SAT BESIDE JENNY'S BED. relating the day's news with her usual bravado.

"It's nice of you to come over," Jenny smiled at the big woman. "You must have sensed this rain had dampened my spirits as well." She turned to stare at the cold raindrops splashing her bedroom window.

"You know I like visitin' with you, honey. How's your arm?"

"Much better. The doctor just wanted me to rest another day."

"You do just that now." Maude's lips quirked in a teasing smile. "Thought that Kincaid feller was never gonna leave."

The glow of love lit Jenny's eyes. "He's been so kind. But he's wasted enough time here. I insisted he get back to work."

"Did they catch that varmint Benson?" Maude scowled.

"No, he got away again," Jenny sighed, "but the Sheriff thinks he'll be easier to track this time."

"Hmph! The Sheriff oughta call in a federal posse. He's got his own hands full keeping law and order here. Ever since he forbid guns on the street . . ." she broke off as Jenny's eyes shifted back to the raindrops. "Remember how I told you to find a man of means?" she asked abruptly. "Well, it seems you have!"

Jenny stared curiously at Maude. "If you're referring to Clint, he is a man of means, as you put it. But it takes more than money to make a person happy. Or so I believe."

"Oh shucks, honey. I know that. Look at me and Ed. We never had money, and we've had a mighty hard life. But we've always had love."

Jenny stared up at the big woman whose glowing eyes illuminated her aging face. For a moment, Jenny could glimpse the pretty girl Maude had once been, back on the Kansas plains.

"Well," Maude cut through Jenny's wandering thoughts. "I hear tell this Kincaid is a fine man. A bit on the wild side, maybe, but you could tame him, Jenny."

"Oh, Maude," Jenny laughed in spite of herself. "I wouldn't try to tame him! In fact, there's very little I would change about Clint. Perhaps that's been the problem," she mused thoughtfully.

"What do you mean?"

"Well, Clint thought I had a lot of ideals that he could never live up to. At least that's what he said. I suppose some men would try to pretend to be something they're not. I have heard women complain of that. But Clint has been honest with me—and with himself. Right now, his main goal in life is to establish his own mining business. To accomplish something on

135

his own. I didn't understand that at first. I thought he just wanted to make a lot of money. But too late I realized that he has to be his own man. And that isn't so bad," her voice trailed away as her eyes lifted to the window to stare out at the aspens, deepening to a blazing gold. It made Jenny sad to watch them being snatched from the trees by gusts of wind, then washed down into soggy piles beneath the fierce onslaught of rain.

She sighed, snuggling deeper into the covers. She still felt very tired, although her encounter with Benson was four days ago.

"Maybe I'll go now and let you rest," Maude patted her shoulder affectionately. "Take care, honey."

Jenny nodded sleepily, watching her go. "Yes, I will. Goodbye Maude — and thank you."

Almost as soon as the front door closed, Jenny was sleeping again, dreaming of a golden-haired man with a beguiling smile.

Jenny's arm healed quickly, and in a matter of days, she was whole again. Except for the pain in her heart. Two weeks had passed since she had seen Clint. He hadn't even come to town for her father's Sunday services. Her pride vied with her arguments in his defense. He had explained when he left that he would have to work long and hard at the mine, making every day count before the bad weather set in.

But didn't *she* count? she wondered sadly. Didn't he care enough to check on her recovery?

She was strolling back from town one afternoon, lost in thought, when a voice greeted her from her front yard. She blinked in confusion at Harvey

Moore, the pleasant young bachelor who had been coming to church.

"Hello, Harvey," she smiled, glancing at the gelding he was hitching to their rail. "Did you need to see my father?"

"Actually, I came to see it you." He gave her a shy smile.

"Oh," Jenny mumbled, taken by surprise.

Harvey was a likeable man in his late twenties who had moved up from Colorado Springs to open a small hardware store. He was thin and tall with an angular body and face and wide-set brown eyes that reflected his honest forthright approach.

A smile crossed her lips as she looked at him. He was neat, well-dressed and cultured. Why couldn't she settle for a wholesome man like Harvey Moore, she wondered, assessing him openly.

"Won't you come in?" she asked, as he shifted from one foot to the other, obviously wondering why she stood there regarding him curiously.

The sweet aroma of Jenny's cinnamon rolls filled the cabin as they stepped inside. Her father looked up from his book at the young man who stood hesitantly in the doorway.

"Harvey! Do come in and warm yourself by the fire. It's a fierce day outside."

"Yes sir, it is." Harvey removed his hat and swept a hand through the wavy brown hair.

"Would you like some coffee and a sweet roll?" Jenny asked, removing her cape.

"That would be wonderful, Miss Jenny." He sniffed the air and a wide smile spread over his thin face. "Sure smells good in here. I miss home cooking." He looked back at Joseph. "I lived with my parents in Colorado Springs, and this is the first time I've tried bachelor life. It has its difficulties," he grinned, crossing to the fire.

Jenny hurried into the kitchen and checked the coffee. Her thoughts lingered on Harvey, and she realized that he had been sizing her up as a candidate for marriage. She sighed, pouring the coffee. He was such a nice man. Why couldn't she feel something for him?

Her heart sank as the truth whispered through her consciousness. *Clint Kincaid.* As she placed the sweet roll on a china plate, she recalled the pleased expression on her father's face when he saw Harvey. She knew her father secretly nurtured a hope that she and Harvey would grow fond of each other.

She took the food to the living room, glancing at Harvey again. Maybe she could learn to love him, she thought, handing him the plate. A man like Harvey was steady and reliable, an easy companion. She sighed, settling into the rocking chair.

"Miss Jenny, this absolutely melts in my mouth," he raved, relishing each bite.

'Thank you," she murmured, her eyes flicking to her father.

Joseph was looking at her, his head tilted in that observant expression he wore when trying to discern someone's thoughts.

"What were you reading, Father?" she asked, determined to distract him from his analysis.

He snapped the book closed. "Just poetry. You know your mother loved poetry."

Jenny's eyes widened on her father. Was he reading poems and thinking of her mother? "Yes, you've told me mother liked poetry." It was hard to imagine

138

loving like that, a love that even death could not destroy.

Something deep in her heart began to ache, and unwillingly she thought of Clint, recalling the poem she had read to him . . . and the kiss that followed!

Suddenly she realized that Harvey had asked her a question.

"Oh, I'm sorry." She sat upright, blinking at him. "I fear the warm fire is making me lazy."

Harvey's eager smile was forgiving. "I asked if you would like to have supper with me at the hotel."

"Oh." Jenny glanced at her father. "I don't think I could do that tonight, Harvey. I have some mending to finish."

"I'm sorry," he dropped his gaze, unable to mask the disappointment on his face.

Staring at his downcast face, she was touched with compassion. "Maybe another time," she offered with a smile.

"Of course!" His head snapped up. "Perhaps one evening next week."

The evening next week came all too soon for Jenny.

As they sat in the hotel dining room, feasting on a sumptuous meal, Jenny fixed a polite expression on her face and tried to appear interested in Harvey's conversation. All the while, her mind wandered back to meals she had taken here with Clint.

"Did you hear about the Lucky Dollar clearing the dance floor last night for a boxing match?" His large brown eyes were filled with humor. "There's never a dull moment in this town, is there?"

"No, there isn't," she answered, glancing across the crowded dining room. Suddenly her gaze met and locked with a pair of brilliant turquoise eyes. She swallowed, trying to pull free, but she found, to her horror, that she could not.

It was only Harvey's repeated question that broke the spell.

"I asked if you cared for dessert," he repeated patiently.

"Oh, no thank you, Harvey." She allowed her smile to become wider than ever. Suddenly, she was alive again, exhilarated by the knowledge of Clint's presence in the room.

Her blinding smile had momentarily struck Harvey dumb. He sat gaping, unable to respond to the waiter who shifted nervously, awaiting a reply.

"No, thank you," she turned to the waiter.

When he moved on, the empty space provided an opening for Jenny to flick a glance toward Clint again. He had pushed his chair back and was striding toward their table.

Her dark head spun back to Harvey, while she mentally assessed her wardrobe for the evening. She had chosen to wear another one of Rebecca's dresses. This was a mauve silk, one that deepened her violet eyes to a dusky velvet, and made her fair skin appear as soft as a rose petal.

"How long has your family lived in Colorado Springs?" she stammered, staring at Harvey.

Harvey had just launched into a story of his childhood when Clint appeared at their table.

"Hello, Jenny."

"Hello, Clint." Harvey was gaping at the intruder. "Harvey, may I present Clint Kincaid, a friend of ours?" Jenny smiled. "Clint, this is Harvey Moore. He recently opened the hardware store at the end of Bennett Avenue."

The men shook hands and Clint lingered. "Then I shall be stopping in to look over your new store." Clint had obviously decided to be charming. "I have a mine up in the foothills and I'm working night and day to make it produce." The words were spoken with deliberation.

"Are you making any progress?" The question was more sarcastic than she intended.

"As a matter of fact, I am!" The blue eyes glowed with satisfaction. "I brought in an ore sample this afternoon that looks very promising."

"Oh." Jenny pushed a curly tendril from her face and smiled. She wished she could force some enthusiasm into her voice. What was wrong with her anyway? She If he were able to strike it rich, she should be happy for him.

"How interesting. How long have you been mining here?" Harvey had taken up the conversation, filling the silence created by the tension between Clint and Jenny.

"A few months." Clint turned back to Harvey. "Well, very nice meeting you," he bowed politely. "Good night."

"Good night," Jenny murmured, watching him walk away.

The wounded look in her violet eyes was lost on Harvey, who had launched into more local news.

Jenny stared at Harvey, thinking. He was such a nice man—honest, considerate, hard-working.

"Harvey, I'm so glad you invited me to supper tonight," she smiled at him, wondering if it were possible to grow to love him. If so, there might be a future with Harvey Moore, after all. Clint Kincaid was slipping out of her life, and she must force herself to face that fact.

CHAPTER 11

"JENNY, WAIT A MINUTE!" Maude yelled as Jenny placed a pot of chicken soup on the kitchen table then prepared to leave.

"Maude, I thought you were sleeping," Jenny sauntered over to peer into the tiny bedroom.

"Just dozing," Maude yawned. "I'm almost over this blasted cold so you can stop waitin' on me, Jenny. You've been such an angel. Can you stay and chat, honey?"

"Sorry, Maude," Jenny smiled. "Harvey Moore is coming for dinner, and I must hurry to the grocery."

Maude frowned. "Harvey Moore?"

"A new merchant in Cripple Creek. He's very nice."

"Hmmm," Maude was studying her carefully. "*Nice*," she repeated. "Do you like him?"

"I'm very fond of him," Jenny responded, her eyes dropping before Maude's penetrating stare. There was no fooling Maude! She could read her like a book. But

142

today, she did not feel inclined toward a lengthy discussion on her finding herself "a man of means."

"Well, I really must go," Jenny said, hurrying across the room.

"What's happened to Clint Kincaid?" Maude's question caught her at the door.

"How should I know?" Jenny responded crossly. "I suppose he's buried himself in his mine. That seems to be all he cares about."

"Jenny?"

She took a deep breath, wishing to avoid an argument with Maude, yet knowing she could not maintain a pleasant facade when her heart was ready to burst.

Maude stood in the doorway of her bedroom, belting her robe tightly about her thick body. "You've changed," she said, pushing a heavy strand of gray hair from her face. "You're seeing what life is all about, honey. Sometimes that hurts."

Jenny sighed, thinking. "My experience with Benson changed me—yes. I've never known anyone so hard and cold and unfeeling. But," she took a deep breath, trying to remain optimistic, "I did try to plant a few seeds of faith while I was at it. Who knows? They may take root and sprout."

"Could be," Maude agreed. "Anyway, I'm glad you've learned that not everybody is as honest as you and yore pa." Disillusionment flickered in Maude's tearful eyes, causing Jenny to wonder about Maude and the things that had happened to destroy her trust.

"I know what you're saying, Maude. I know that we are tested so that we can be strengthened in faith. But we do have to believe in people, don't we? We have to care and hope and . . . keep on praying. Even if we are disappointed, we should find a way to grow from our experiences."

"That's right," Maude's head wagged in agreement. "When I said you had changed, I guess I mean you had grown. You know how the miners test their gold?" she asked suddenly. "They put the gold in the fire! If it's real, it comes out strong and pure. Maybe we are put through the fire to see what we're made of. Ever thought of that, Jenny?"

Jenny's smooth brow puckered in thought. "I never thought of it quite that way. Maude," her eyes brightened with an idea, "you've just given me a very good topic for my next Bible class. The ladies who come to my class know about life's difficulties. They can relate to your parable of gold in the fire, and a person's struggles and heartaches. Thanks, Maude." Her smile widened.

"I thought we was talkin' about Clint Kincaid," Maude laughed. "How did we get off on your Bible class?"

"We were talking about heartache. And I'm afraid the word reminds me of Clint Kincaid! See you later, Maude." She whirled and hurried out the door before Maude could say more.

Last week's rain had ended, and the town was enjoying a few days of compensating sunshine. Jenny pulled her cape about her and set off down the hill to the grocery.

Her father was still delivering for Warren and Williams, and it was because he was on one of his runs this very day that she was forced to hasten down for some staples she needed in her baking.

As she rounded the corner of Bennett Avenue, Clint's fawn stallion, hitched to the rail before the bath house, caught her eye. She hesitated in front of the horse, wishing the big stallion could answer some questions concerning his master. She turned and cast a brief glance toward the closed door of the bath house, then sauntered on.

"Jenny!"

Whirling at the sound of his voice, she confronted a clean, freshly-shaven Clint. He was dressed in a new buckskin jacket, clean trousers, and gleaming leather boots. As usual, he wore no hat, and the crown of golden sun-bleached hair accented his bronze face and luminous blue eyes.

"Hello,' she tilted her head back, forcing a smile.

"Could I buy you a cup of coffee at the bakery?" he asked hopefully. "I have some exciting news!"

Jenny hesitated. She hadn't the time to dawdle, since Harvey was coming for a dinner not yet prepared. Still, she couldn't resist hearing Clint's news.

"All right, but I haven't much time," she insisted as he grasped her arm and steered her through the door of the cozy bakery.

Jenny sniffed the rich aroma of yeast and coffee, and a pang of hunger struck her.

"How have you been?" Clint asked, studying her curiously.

She glanced back at him, acutely aware of his hand on her arm.

"Fine," she replied, then frowned up at him. "No, actually I haven't been fine," she admitted. "I've been worried about your working out in that awful rain last week. How did you escape your death of cold?"

Clint chuckled, as though he were immune to

inclement weather. "When you're working underground, you are shielded from the elements—to a certain extent." He pulled a chair back for her. "I have something to tell you," he reached across the table to grasp her hand.

"What is it?"

"I've struck a deep vein of gold! Tomorrow I'm going to Denver to see my father. It appears I may have one of the richest mines in the area!"

"That's wonderful!" Jenny exclaimed, forgetting her irritation with him. This time she, too, was seized with the undercurrent of excitement. "Your father will be so pleased, Clint."

"Yes," he glanced at the waitress who was placing the strong black coffee before them. "It's what I've worked for, had hoped would happen. Jenny, I couldn't go back empty-handed."

Jenny leaned back in the chair, staring at the radiant man before her. The blue eyes that she had once likened to a clear Colorado sky were filled with hope and promise.

"Well, what do you think?" His fingers pressed her hand.

She looked back at him and smiled. "I think I am *very* happy for you. How do you plan to market your gold?"

He sipped his coffee. "That's one of the things I want to discuss with my father. I want him to be included in the decisions."

Jenny nodded with approval. "That's a good idea."

"Jenny, can you spend the rest of the day with me? I'd like to be with you. There are some things I want to tell you . . ." he broke off, seeing the quick, negative toss of her head.

"I'm sorry, Clint. Harvey Moore is coming for supper this evening."

He released her fingers and stared into his coffee cup. "Harvey Moore," he repeated dully.

Some of the brilliant glow seemed to have faded from the intent blue eyes.

"Well, I have not been very attentive to you lately. I realize that," he admitted, a note of reserve in his voice. "But this is a very special day for me. I wanted to share it with someone special."

His gaze met hers, and for a moment she was lost in the quiet pleading of his eyes.

"Clint," she swallowed, "Harvey has been very nice to me. I musn't be unkind."

"I see," he tilted his coffee cup to drain its contents. "Then I won't detain you."

Impulsively, she reached across the table and grasped his hand. "Please don't pout. Since you haven't been around lately, I thought perhaps," she hesitated, summoning her courage to be honest, "you didn't care to see me anymore."

"Of course I want to see you." He took a deep breath and studied her slim fingers entwined in his strong ones. "And I'm still very sorry you were involved in my dealings with Benson. But," he shrugged, "he's still living on the run, probably jumping at his own shadow. Even though we didn't catch him, I think he's created his own punishment."

"I think so too," she agreed. Then suddenly she remembered her errand, and reluctantly, she pulled free of his hand. "Clint, I must go."

He leaned back in the chair, hooking his thumbs in his vest. "Are you serious about this Moore fellow?" he asked.

She pushed her chair back and stood up. Her violet eyes dropped to his inquiring face, considering his question. She decided it was time Clint Kincaid stopped taking her for granted.

"I don't know," she responded, offering him only a half smile in parting. "Good day, Clint."

She could feel the weight of his shock as she strolled out the door and left him sitting alone at the table.

Jenny suffered through what seemed an endless evening with Harvey Moore. She had tried desperately to be polite, to smile and look interested, to say all the right things, to ask the right questions. When he finally said good night, she almost moaned in relief.

Long after her father had retired for the night, she sat staring into the fire, unable to sleep. And then a tapping sounded at the door, so light that, at first, she thought she might only have imagined it.

Yet the tapping came again, soft and persistent. No doubt, a member of the congregation with a problem. Before she disturbed her father, she would see who was there—and if she could help.

She lifted the curtain and her eyes widened. A fawn stallion was tied to the hitching rail. Clint!

Hurrying to the door, she paused. "Clint?" she called softly.

"Jenny, could I speak with you for a moment?"

She unlatched the door and peered curiously into the lean face above her.

"I . . . I'm sorry to bother you," he said, looking deeply troubled.

"It's no bother," she opened the door and stepped aside. "Come in. Father is already asleep. However, if you need to speak with him—"

"It's you I came to speak with," he interrupted, his eyes sweeping her thoughtfully.

She closed the door softly, then turned to face him. With her delicate face tilted and the violet eyes enormous with unspoken questions, Clint thought his heart might leap from his chest. With great effort, he tore his gaze away and stalked toward the fire, trying to collect his thoughts, so that his words did not tumble out as senselessly as the school boy he now felt himself to be.

He spread his fingers before the fire, warming them, as Jenny moved to his side, waiting.

She tried to still her pounding heart, reminding herself that this was the man who had hurt her, who could not be depended upon, whose life centered around his gold mine. She was curious, though, as to what had prompted this late-night visit.

"What did you want to talk about, Clint?" she asked patiently.

He turned slowly, casting a worried glance at her. "About you . . . me . . . us."

" Us ?" she echoed, dropping into the rocking chair to support her suddenly weak knees. There was no predicting what Clint Kincaid might say or do. When she was so certain he was angry with her, or had lost interest in her, he appeared again.

"Jenny," he began, and stopped. He took a deep breath and shoved his hands in his pockets. "You've been very kind to me. You have shown me more understanding and compassion than any woman I've ever known." The blue eyes reflected the tenderness of his words. He paused, studying the confused expression on her face. "I have deliberately avoided you these past weeks because . . . ."

He glanced nervously around the small living room, apparently gathering the courage to forge on. "In the beginning, I didn't feel I could possibly measure up to your expectations of a man. Yours or your father's. When I started attending church again, I found myself changing, little by little. It will take time, as I have warned you before. But I do want to be a better person because . . ."

"Go on," she prompted, watching him with a mixture of curiosity and fascination. She had never seen him so unsure of himself, so vulnerable — not even when he lay ill on their hearth. Even then, there had been a kind of stubborn determination that dominated his responses.

"Because I'm falling in love with you," his voice dropped to a husky whisper.

She felt a sharp intake of breath, astonishment widening her violet eyes.

"I know I haven't behaved like a man in love—or maybe I have," he shrugged. "This is all so new to me. I have never felt this way before."

Jenny couldn't believe what she was hearing. She stared down at her tightly-gripped fingers, struggling to calm her racing thoughts.

"I want to please you," he was studying her thoughtfully, "and yet I have to be myself."

"Of course you have to be yourself, Clint. You could never be dishonest or hypocritical."

"And I still feel that you are, well, too trusting," he added softly. "Perhaps if you hadn't been, though, you might never have allowed me back on your doorstep."

"Why are you telling me this now?"

"Because, I don't want you to do something foolish—like marry Harvey Moore."

"Foolish?" she countered. "Harvey Moore is a very good man. I hardly think anyone who chooses him for a husband will be making a foolish decision."

"You would be," he reached down for her hand, and gently pulled her to him.

"And why is that?" she mumbled, mesmerized by the blue eyes that traveled from her eyes to her nose to her parted lips.

"Because I think you feel the same way I do," he said, his lips dipping to claim hers.

The kiss was urgent and demanding, more passionate than she had expected.

She drew back from him, suddenly frightened by the intensity of his emotions.

"Please wait, Clint." She pressed her small hands against his jacket, gently pushing him away. "I do have feelings for you, but I am not yet certain how to label them. You have left me confused, frustrated, and maybe a bit disillusioned. And until now, you haven't given me much indication that you . . . loved me," she almost choked on the words.

"Jenny," his arms tightened around her shoulders, "What do I have to do to make you understand? Would I come barging in at this hour if I were not serious? Would I have waited up the road for the past two hours, watching for Harvey to leave so that I could speak to you?"

She broke free and stepped back, anger flaring in her dark gaze. "You have had plenty of chances, Clint. Why were you so eager to see me tonight? Is it because you can't abide the thought of some other man taking your girl?" She knew her words were cruel and unfair, though possibly true. She could not seem to stop herself. "Do you really love me, Clint? Or are you merely trying to prove something again?"

A cold light flickered in his eyes as the lean jaw hardened.

"Do you have any idea how hard it was for me to admit my feelings to you?" he asked tightly.

"Why? It has been hard for me not to conceal mine. You know how I feel about you, and yet you've kept me waiting and wondering, never certain what you were going to do next!"

"I shouldn't have come," he muttered under his breath and strode toward the door.

Her lips parted and a protest formed in her mind. But it was a protest she could not voice. She wanted him to leave so she could sort out her feelings.

She watched the door close softly, and she stood staring for a long moment, wondering why she did not stop him.

She loved Clint, there was no denying the truth. And it was unlikely that she would ever feel such a strong bond for another man. But she felt affection for Harvey—and respect. True, unlike the charming, unpredictable Clint Kincaid he was almost boring. Nevertheless she had come to appreciate the steady, safe relationship Harvey offered.

Was that what she wanted—a marriage in which she would always know what to expect—and what not to expect?

"Jenny?" her father's door opened, and he stood there, his head tilted in that keen, observant manner he had. "I couldn't help overhearing what Clint said. How are you feeling, my dear little girl?"

Her large eyes were filled with hurt. "Father, I love him. I cannot deny it. But I'm . . . afraid of a future with him."

"And you are wise to be cautious," he nodded.

"Jenny, I couldn't bear to see you hurt." He lifted a thin hand to rake through his tousled dark hair. He strolled over to the fireplace and lifted a poker to prod a dwindling flame. In doing so, he seemed to be searching his mind for the right words to say to her. "I would be happy to see you settle down with Harvey Moore," he said quietly.

"I know," she sighed. "Harvey is a fine Christian man. But . . . ." her voice trailed away, as she sank into the rocking chair again.

"Give yourself time, Jenny." Her father smiled down with understanding. "God will guide you. You must have faith in His ability to do that."

"Oh, Father, I know He will, but the waiting is so hard, and I'm so confused!" Her face was contorted with her suffering and she flew to her father's side to nestle her head on his shoulder. "What would I do without you, Father? I love you so much!"

He gave her an awkward pat and cleared his throat noisily. "And I love you, too, daughter. It will be hard to let you go."

"Now, Father," she laughed, brushing a hand over a tear-stained cheek, "I'm not going anywhere! Neither man has asked for my hand in marriage!"

"But it will happen," he said with sudden conviction. "Yes, they will be asking very soon, I fear."

CHAPTER 12

"IT'S A PERFECT STAR," Jenny said surveying the hand-made ornament atop the blue spruce. "How sweet of little Tommy to make it for us."

"He hasn't forgotten those games of checkers you played with him," Joseph glanced across at his daughter, as he stepped back from the tree to admire their handiwork.

On his last errand into the mountains for Warren and Williams, he had located the full blue spruce, standing alone on a hillside, begging to be taken home for Christmas. Jenny had taken over as soon as the tree was angled through the narrow door, working day and night with a kind of childish fervor. She had strung red berries and pine cones, chains of popcorn, and added the hand-painted wooden ornaments, brought out from St. Louis.

"I still say we're rushing the season a bit," he looked at her with an amused twinkle in his brown eyes. "This is only the second day of December."

"Oh no, we're not!" Jenny clasped her hands before her and lifted her radiant face to the tree, violet eyes sparkling with joy.

"Well," Joseph dusted his hands and turned for his coat, "I must hurry on to the deacons' meeting. We must decide how best to distribute fruit and toys to the needy."

"Mmmm," Jenny nodded, her eyes never leaving the tree.

"Is Harvey dropping by tonight?"

Suddenly the lovely moment was spoiled, and a shadow crossed Jenny's face. She bit her lip. "I suppose so." Harvey was making a habit of dropping in quite regularly. At first, Jenny had welcomed his visits to help ease the loneliness of losing Clint again. But now her conscience had begun to nag at her, warning her that it was wrong to encourage Harvey in this way if she did not return his love. For it was common knowledge that Harvey was in love with her, and the only flaw in the approach of Christmas day was the decision whether or not to accept the ring he would undoubtedly offer her.

"Jenny," Joseph touched her arm, pulling her from her confused daze, "you must be fair to Harvey. And you must be fair to yourself."

She turned worried eyes to her father. "How can I do that?"

"I don't know," he sighed, shoving his arms through his coat. "I just wish I could see that old sparkle in your eyes. You love Clint Kincaid, don't you?"

Jenny looked into the troubled face of her father, wishing with all of her heart she could deny it. Her father had been so pleased to have Harvey around, and she knew it had been one of his greatest desires to see her settled down with Harvey to a comfortable future as his wife and the mother of his children. But the spark of love she had so diligently prayed for had not come, and now she doubted that it would. So she was left with a tormenting decision to marry for security—or love.

Her father was striding to the door when she realized she still had not answered his question. Perhaps now she would be spared that embarrassment.

"Perhaps we can discuss it later, Father," she called after him in a tone of apology.

"Good night," he glanced back at her, the troubled expression still present in his dark eyes.

As he closed the door, she sank into the rocking chair and stared into the flickering fire. *Why couldn't she get Clint out of her mind?* Surely this was not a cross she must bear for the rest of her life! She had tried so hard to fall in love with Harvey, and even though she admired and respected him, he was still just a friend.

Watching the flames dance before her, she thought of the many marriages of convenience during pioneer days, and even here in Cripple Creek. Was it being too idealistic to hold out for an emotion that lifted you above the dull routine of everyday life and transported you to some wondrous place? Perhaps it was. One didn't build a marriage on that kind of emotion—feelings that must wear thin with time. And yet . . . she heaved a weary sigh . . . and yet when things were going well with Clint, it seemed her feet never touched the ground. The cares and drudgeries of life were somehow dimmed in the radiance of their being together.

A brisk knock on the door ended her reflection, and she pulled herself up with new resolve. It was time she freed herself of schoolgirl fantasies and faced reality. She was fortunate to have a man like Harvey! Everyone told her that real love did not come until one shared hardships and happiness, children, and years of being together.

She forced a welcoming smile and opened the door, never once imagining that the man she would face would not be Harvey – but Clint!

"Hello, Jenny."

Her breath ceased for a moment as her eyes widened on the well-dressed gentleman towering above her. He was dressed in a black top-hat, a dark suit and black leather boots. He appeared to be in good health and the blue eyes held an enigmatic glow as he looked down at her.

"Hello, Clint," she swallowed, suddenly remembering her manners. "Won't you come in?"

As he removed his hat and stepped inside, the plain little room was transformed by his presence. There was an aura about him that changed everything. Her heartbeat quickened, and she found herself drawn to him in the same old way, drawn with a force she could not ignore.

"What a pretty tree!" Clint's face lit up with pleasure.

"Father says I'm rushing the season. Most folks don't put up their trees this early."

"Fear of fire, I suppose."

"I've always been early with ours." Jenny sighed. "There's so much joy and hope at Christmas," she cast a nostalgic glance at he tree, "that I can't resist getting into the spirit as soon as possible."

They stood in silence for a moment, looking at the tree. Then Jenny turned back to him, suddenly wondering why he had come.

"Would you like some coffee?" she asked nervously.

"No, thank you." He had removed his hat and was about to unbutton his coat. "Were you expecting someone?" he asked, as she glanced toward the door.

Her eyes dropped to the hat in his hand as she pondered a reply. "Harvey usually stops by in the evenings," she admitted, 'but you don't have to leave now."

"I see." Pride sharpened his tone. Automatically, his back stiffened as he unbuttoned the overcoat and hooked it over the coat tree. "Then I won't stay long."

"How was Denver?" she asked, taking a seat opposite him. She assumed that's where he had been these past weeks, although one could never be sure with Clint.

"Very pleasant," he smiled, momentarily forgetting about Harvey, "and profitable I would say. At last, I feel my parents understand the goals that have driven me—and I have come to appreciate them, as well. They're good and loving people." The glow in his eyes confirmed his happiness. "Jenny, I came to invite you to return with me on the weekend. My mother would like to meet you."

Jenny blinked in surprise. Go to Denver to meet his mother? Then the memory of their conversation at the Nellie B cleared her confusion. She had expressed a desire, on that day, to meet his mother. Circumstances had been different then—she had dared hope Clint shared her love. But now everything had changed.

"Jenny, do you think your father would permit it?" Clint pressed, eager for her answer. We could go up on the train . . ." he broke off as she shook her dark head.

"Clint, I'm much too busy preparing for Christmas," Jenny replied. "The choir will be presenting a program of music, and we're practicing this weekend. Also, I have my baking to do, and there's my Bible class," she broke off, remembering Kate. "Did you happen to see Kate while you were home?" she asked quickly.

"No, I didn't. But my mother mentioned that she had returned, and that she and her family are working out their differences."

"I'm so glad," Jenny breathed a sigh of relief.

"I told my mother about you," Clint said. "How you had helped me, and Kate, and so many others. Jenny, I owe you an apology—for many things." The blue eyes filled with a look of regret.

Jenny shook her head quickly. "It's all right, Clint. We come from different worlds. Perhaps that's why it has been difficult for me to understand you."

"And for me to understand you," he sighed, turning to stare into the fire.

For a moment, each was lost in thought, and then slowly Clint's blue eyes slipped back to her, a quiet plea in their depths.

"Give me another chance, Jenny," he said, his voice little more than a whisper. "I'll prove to you that I can make you happy—can be the right man for you."

"Clint, you don't understand," Jenny protested. "You don't have to be right for *me*. You have to be your own man—you told me that long ago, and I agree. But that isn't what bothers me."

"Then what is it?"

"Our attitudes are different. You don't understand my commitment to helping people here."

"And you don't understand my indifference," he nodded in understanding. "Don't you see, Jenny? Now that my mining operation is underway, I can be in church on Sundays. I wasn't trying to make a god of my mine, but time was running out for me. I knew if I didn't strike gold soon —" his voice trailed away as a look of despair filled his eyes.

"But you know how strongly I feel about carrying out my mission here to Cripple Creek. My father and I are committed to helping these people in any way we can. You think that is . . ." she lifted a hand in an effort to explain her thoughts.

"I believe the word was idealistic," he said with a wry grin.

"Yes, idealistic," she repeated sadly. "Even in the matter of Benson."

He nodded then heaved a sigh. "I seem to be compelled in a different direction. Doing for *myself*, which must seem very selfish to you. But I believe I've learned a lesson merely from watching *you*. You see, I've never met anyone like you and your father. My parents are Christians but they aren't committed to people the way you and your father are. I don't know," he shook his head in an effort to clear his mind, "you just seem so sweet and fragile and innocent. I guess," he looked back in tenderness, "I have been trying to protect you from the harsh realities of the world. But as you pointed out during our last argument, you may know more of reality than I. I'm sorry, Jenny."

"Clint, will you please stop apologizing?" she leapt

out of the chair and began to pace the floor. "It doesn't suit you," she glanced at him anxiously, "and it really isn't necessary."

"Then what will it take?" his eyes followed her.

"What do you mean?"

"What will it take to persuade you to give me another chance?"

A soft tapping on the front door interrupted her answer. "Your company has arrived," Clint sighed and stood up. "Will you have lunch with me tomorrow?"

"Of course," she smiled, watching helplessly as he strolled over to get his coat. The tapping became more persistent and this time he cast an angry glare toward the door.

"I'll see you tomorrow," she smiled up into his face. "Why don't you come around noon."

He nodded and turned for the door. Then, as if suddenly remembering something, he swung around and planted a kiss on her lips. "That will give you something to think about while you're entertaining what's-his-name. Good night."

The evening dragged on interminably as Jenny sat with Harvey, forcing herself not to fidget as he related events of his day at the store.

This is how it would be, she thought, with a flash of panic. If we were married, we would sit before the fire and he would tell me news of his day. I would be knitting or sewing or rocking the baby . . . . Suddenly all the joy she had experienced earlier drained away, and she felt lifeless and old beyond her years.

It occurred to her that Harvey had stopped talking and was studying her curiously.

"Jenny, you haven't heard a word I've been saying, have you?"

She bolted upright, her cheeks flushing. "What? Oh, well I . . ." she faltered beneath his searching gaze, and slowly she shook her head, aware of her preoccupation. "I'm sorry, Harvey," she mumbled, her eyes dropping to her hands, folded in her lap. There was nothing more she could say. Why pretend?

"Jenny, I know what's bothering you. It's that Kincaid fellow, isn't it? I know you care about him."

Her head jerked up in surprise, and her violet eyes slowly betrayed her. Tears were gathering, even though she tried desperately to hold them back.

"Harvey, I don't know what to say," she swallowed, wishing there was some sensible way she could explain her feelings. But love seemed to make no sense at all.

His thin face had paled beneath her silent admission of the truth. He poised on the edge of the sofa, and Jenny dreaded the inevitable confrontation.

"Are you in love with him?" The words fell like stones.

She took a deep breath, silently praying for strength. How could she lie to Harvey? How could she deny her feelings? And yet what good were these feelings when an enduring relationship with Clint was not likely?

The silence stretched between them, as the question hovered in their minds. A small aspen log broke in the fire and hissed into flames.

"Harvey, I respect you far too much to be dishonest. I . . . I had already met Clint Kincaid before you moved here."

"I know," he was nodding. "You and your father cared for him when he was hurt, but . . ."

She lifted a hand to silence the objection that most of the members of the congregation shared.

"He may be a bit . . . different . . .from the rest of us," she sighed. "I've told myself that countless times, and Father has reminded me as well. But that still doesn't change my feelings, Harvey." She shook her head. "I wish I could. I've tried. I've often prayed about it. And sometimes I think I don't care for him anymore, but then," she swallowed, gathering courage to forge on, "then he comes back into my life, and it's as though he had never left. Yes, I do love him, Harvey. I'm sorry."

He stared at her for a long moment and then slowly he got up from the sofa. "I see. Then I am going to stop intruding in your life—at least until you decide what to do."

Jenny jumped to her feet, distraught with the knowledge that her words had wounded him deeply. "Harvey, I can only pray that you understand. You are a fine, wonderful man."

"But you don't love me," the words were flat and cold — and true.

She searched for the right words while she stood mute, staring at him with tears shimmering in her violet eyes.

"It's all right, Jenny," he patted her arm gently. "I suppose a person cannot help how he or she feels. I should know," he mumbled, as he made for the door.

After he left, Jenny stared miserably through the window into the darkness. She had not wanted to hurt Harvey; she should have told him sooner how she felt. But how could she know that Clint would keep reappearing in her life? And how could she know that she was unable to deny herself the opportunity to see him, to be with him just once more?

Would she now give Clint the chance he had asked

for? *Another chance*, he had said. She turned from the window and walked over to stare up at the beauty of the blue spruce, adorned with the simple decorations she had made. Suddenly, the old hope burned within her anew. This was the season of celebrating the birth of Christ. That should be uppermost in her mind now. And it was, in a way. Still, maybe it was significant that Clint had come back during this season of miracles. Maybe somehow God would provide a miracle for them. Maybe their love had a chance, after all.

Jenny and Clint strolled down the crowded sidewalk, fascinated by the many items displayed in the shop windows. All the inhabitants of Cripple Creek, whether believers or not, were looking forward to this reprieve from work and worry, despite the nostalgia some felt for distant homes.

"Are you sure you won't change your mind and come with me to Denver?" Clint asked, for the tenth time.

"I just can't," she replied softly, wishing now that she could dismiss her duties and board the train with him.

He opened the door to the bakery and, drawn by the savory smells, wandered in for a cup of coffee. As he helped her off with her coat, his fingers lingered for a second on her shoulder.

The day had been so wonderful, Jenny thought, recalling how kind and considerate Clint had been. The knowledge that he was returning to Denver for Christmas saddened her, but she tried to maintain a brave facade.

As they sat down at the cozy wooden table,

164

awaiting their coffee, Clint reached across and grasped her small cold hand.

"Jenny, one of the reasons I want you to visit my parents is because I think you could understand me better. You see," his eyes dropped to her small fingers, "I have always stood in my older brother's shadow. Or so it seems to me. William is the perfect son; I, the prodigal. I grew up believing that he was the family pet. He did everything right. I was the rebel. I got into the neighborhood fights, got the spankings at school, spilled the ink on Dad's desk, broke my mother's favorite dish. Need I go on?" he paused, a wry grin chiseling his lips.

Jenny squeezed his hand. "Yes, please do. I'm fascinated."

"Well, there came a time when I had enough of being William's little brother. That occurred when he became Vice President of the lumber company, and again I was expected to fall in line as his subordinate. I just couldn't do it," he shrugged. "I knew it was time to make my own way."

"And you have." Jenny beamed at him with pride.

"Maybe." The blue eyes deepened as he studied her thoughtfully. "I'm going to have to be away from the mine a lot this winter, Jenny. Father and I are going to Europe after Christmas to investigate a new market for our gold."

She could feel her hopes plummeting again. It seemed their time together was destined to be limited. She could even see that as soon as he could staff his mine, Clint would no longer need to live in Cripple Creek.

Clint read the message in her eyes and reached for her other hand. "Listen to me." The urgency in his voice brought her troubled gaze back to his gentle smile. "I have a reason for telling you these things. I want you to understand."

'Why?" she asked. "Why do you feel you need to keep explaining? You already have."

"Because I want you to understand what my future will be. Confusion at first," he admitted with a shrug, "but by the spring I should be able to settle down to a normal life here in Cripple Creek."

"Here?" Jenny repeated blankly.

"Yes, here. I like Cripple Creek and have no desire to live anywhere else. I'm certainly not returning to Denver. My father now respects my wishes, and I've proven to him that my ideas weren't so bad, after all."

Jenny stared at him, trying to absorb the meaning of his words.

"I guess what I'm saying is, as soon as I get the mine going, and as soon as my markets are determined, I will be the image of the respectable church-going husband. Will you marry me, Jenny?"

She gasped in surprise, feeling as though she had just been gently nudged from the top of Pikes Peak. The descent was dizzying, and for a moment she could not recover her breath.

"Are you so surprised?" he laughed. "Surely you knew I would eventually ask you to be my wife?"

She shook her head, her mind spinning. Not in her wildest dreams had she expected such a question to be forthcoming today.

"I know your father has reservations, along with your friends," he continued gently, "but if only they'll give me a chance, if only *you* will give me a chance, I'll make you happy. I promise you, Jenny. I will make you happy! For you see, I love you — very, very, much."

"I believe you do," she stared at him, scarcely able to grasp what was happening. "And I love you, Clint. I have loved you almost from the first moment I saw you. I assumed only the poets believed in love at first sight, but I know now that it is possible."

Clint stared at her, watching the velvet eyes shine with new brilliance. He sighed, dropping his gaze to the dainty hand that clung to his, as though trying to absorb his warmth and physical strength.

"Everything will work out for us, Jenny. We have to believe that," he said with incredible tenderness.

"Yes, I know," she whispered.

The diamond ring that Clint gave Jenny was the talk of Cripple Creek. Myrtle Tubbs searched the Scripture for the appropriate disclaimer to such worldliness. Even Joseph Townley worried that some poverty-striken miner would yank the valuable ring from his daughter's finger. But Jenny was undaunted.

She stared down into the brilliance of the diamond whose glow was matched only by the radiance in her eyes. Clint came to share Christmas with her two days early. Their evening had been spent with a deacon and his wife, Maude and her beloved Sam, Belle, the maid from the hotel, and Joseph Townley. Jenny thrived on the variety of people in her life and had purposely planned this special group for a quiet little supper, then carols sung around the Christmas tree.

Her artistic, hand-made ornaments filled the cabin, and giant evergreen wreaths hung in every window and on the front door. The little log cabin seemed to belong in a storybook, rather than on a hillside above Cripple Creek. Everyone who passed the Townley residence stopped to stare.

And Jenny herself was as shining and radiant as any of her ornaments. Her delicate face gleamed with a new kind of beauty, an inner radiance that sparkled in the depths of her violet eyes and quickened her smile.

As the group sang their last carol, tears filled every female eye. Even the men were strangely quiet.

Clint Kincaid, seated beside Jenny, appeared to be a changed man. The hard sheen that had once filled his eyes was gone now, replaced by a look of tenderness as he looked at Jenny. And he was always looking at her, as though he would never tire of her sweet, smiling face.

Later, when everyone had left, and after Joseph had retired, Jenny and Clint sat alone before the fire.

"Jenny, I want to be a more giving person," he had said to her. "Like you and your father. You do so much for all these people," his arm swept the air, signifying the town beyond their window.

"Clint, I never think about doing," Jenny laughed softly, "because I receive so much joy in return."

He nodded. "I'm going to use some of the money from my gold mine to do something worthwhile. I mean it," his eyes were dark and serious, "wait and see."

Then as the fire dwindled, and happy exhaustion took over, they said goodnight. The next day Clint boarded the train for Denver and Jenny waved to him with a sad smile.

She spent the remaining week in a state of euphoria. Daily, she went to the hospital, taking gifts to those who would otherwise have none. After the choir's special program of Christmas hymns, she hosted a supper at their home, the happy fellowship climaxing a lovely evening. She even hosted a little party for her

Bible class, which had expanded to more than a dozen ladies now.

The worried expression in Joseph's eyes had begun to fade as he watched his daughter, happier than ever, blossoming into the strong and vibrant woman he had always known she would be. Maude watched too, pleased that the wide-eyed, little girl look had been replaced by something more enduring. Now there was an expression of love and gentleness and compassion, and wisdom too, a wisdom that had not been there before.

"I believe that Kincaid feller has been good for Jenny," Maude proclaimed to her husband at the supper table. "It's just like I told her that day she brought me chicken soup. The Good Lord sometimes puts us through the fire to see what we're made of. Jenny got tested, and now she's come out of it stronger than ever."

On Christmas day Joseph Townley received the greatest gift of his entire life. A load of timber and bricks arrived in Cripple Creek, sent from Kincaid Lumber Company in Denver. The message was, "Start building your church. Clint and Calvin Kincaid."

Joseph's astonished refusals were quickly brushed aside, and soon the material was unloaded on the western hillside beyond Cripple Creek, the new land recently acquired by the congregation for the church they hoped to build some day. Someday had suddenly become *now*.

True to his word, Calvin Kincaid had not forgotten what the Townleys had done for his son. And Clint obviously intended to carry out his new resolution to do something for the people of Cripple Creek.

Joseph made an anxious phone call from the bank to Calvin Kincaid in Denver offering to turn the gift into a loan that the church would eventually repay. The offer was kindly refused.

Joseph spent hours walking around the massive pile of lumber and bricks, scratching his head, staring in amazement. His dream was finally going to come true. Cripple Creek was going to have a new church!

In all the merriment and excitement of that December, only one shadow flickered in the background, one that only Jenny noticed and remembered. The wedding date had not been mentioned.

CHAPTER 13

A SNOWSTORM USHERED in the new year, forcing Jenny and her father to cancel all church activities. They spent much of their time talking together about plans for building the church and concerns of the people in their charge.

"Father, how many people do you think have prospered from the gold rush?" Jenny asked, as they sat at the kitchen table sipping coffee.

"Only a few," he said. "Clint may be one of the richest. I understand there may still be millions of dollars in gold beneath the ground. But locating a rich vein of ore and getting it out of the ground is tricky and difficult."

Jenny nodded, recalling Clint's long difficult struggle. "Clint worked very hard for what he has," she responded, her eyes glowing with pride.

"And he is sharing what he has with Cripple Creek." Joseph smiled at his daughter. "I'm glad you held on to your dream, that you settled for no less than true love."

"I do love him," she said with a wistful smile. "But I must wait a little longer before my dream can become a reality."

The waiting stretched on, through snow-filled winter days and long, lonely nights.

Presents arrived almost weekly from Clint postmarked from different parts of the world. A Swiss music box, a porcelain doll from Germany, lace handkerchiefs from Spain. Jenny was thrilled with the gifts, but there were many times when she would have eagerly exchanged all of them for just one letter from him. Just *one*.

In April, robins and bluebirds began drifting into the valley, signaling the approach of spring. And with the first warm days, volunteer workers broke ground for the new church.

Jenny tried to keep herself occupied with sewing, baking, and church activities, but a deep sadness had taken root in her heart. It seemed that Clint had been gone forever, and without him her life was not complete.

On the twenty-fifth day of April, Joseph Townley's birthday, Jenny planned to surprise her father with a special lunch at the hotel. She quickly hid her disappointment, however, when she learned that Susan Barkley, an attractive widow in their congregation, had invited him to partake of yet another of her sumptuous meals.

"She's an extraordinary lady, Jenny," Joseph boasted. "She came over here from Scotland so that her husband could fulfill a lifelong dream. But he died of a heart attack on their second day in Cripple Creek. Mrs. Barkley lacked the funds to return home."

"That must have been difficult for her," Jenny murmured, recalling the quiet, dark-haired woman. "But," she added with a smile, "you two seem to be good for each other. You've gained a few pounds this past month."

He laughed, putting a hand to his stomach. "It's those rich custard pies she bakes. Any coffee?"

"Yes, of course," she grinned at him, aware that he wanted to change the subject. Her father was in love! And the fact that he was shy about the relationship touched Jenny's heart. She wanted him to be happy and she knew he had grieved long enough for her mother.

Still, after he left for Mrs. Barkley's home, Jenny paced through the cabin, feeling more alone than ever. She sank into a chair, trying to divert her thoughts from Clint, but it seemed impossible.

An urgent tapping at her door brought her quickly to her feet. As always, her hopes soared, even while knowing the caller could not possibly be Clint.

A small, dark man made a quick swipe for his felt hat. "Mornin' ma'am. Belle sent me to fetch you. She's right poorly this morning. She wondered if you would come and sit with her for a spell."

"Yes, of course." Jenny reached for her shawl. "Thank you for coming."

She followed the man back down the hill to the weathered, clapboard boarding house where Belle had a room on the top floor.

As Jenny entered the building and climbed the rickety stairs, her heart went out to Belle who worked long, hard hours cleaning the rooms at the hotel, then had to make this tiring climb each evening. She finally reached the top floor and tapped softly on Belle's door. When she heard a muffled response she opened the door and peered inside.

The room was small and sparsely furnished with a horsehair settee and two chairs at one end, and an iron bed and chest at the other.

"Jenny!" Belle sat up in bed, her ashen face reflecting sudden joy. "Bless you for coming."

Jenny tried to conceal her worry beneath a smile.

"What's wrong, Belle," she asked, pulling a chair up to the bed.

"Just a bad cold. But I been having some pains in my chest. I kinda thought you might say a prayer for me."

"Of course I will, Belle." Jenny touched her hand. "Then why don't you let me make arrangements for you to go to the hospital. I think you need a doctor," she added gently.

Belle gave an adamant toss of her head. "I ain't going to the hospital. If I'm gonna die, I'd rather die right here in my own bed."

"Belle! You aren't going to die." Jenny smiled at her. "But you do need some medicine."

"*Fire!*" A hoarse shout rose from the street below them. Jenny stiffened, wondering if she had heard correctly.

"*Fire! Fire!*"

Belle grasped her arm. "What is it? What are they yelling about?"

Jenny dashed to the window, then gasped in shock.

Smoke was billowing from the roof of the three story dance hall, directly across the street. Flames were shooting from open windows where the wind snatched the embers and dashed them onto the adjoining roofs.

174

For a moment, Jenny was paralyzed with fear. Her hands gripped the window sill as she scanned the crowded street. Volunteer firefighters were urging the girls trapped on the top floor of the burning buiding to jump from the window down onto the canvas they had stretched out below. Flames crackled and timbers caved in, as the fire spread with lightening speed.

"Belle, we have to get out of here!" Jenny raced over to toss the covers back from the startled woman. "The buildings across the street are on fire. It's only a matter of minutes until the fire spreads here." She paused, glancing at the thin pine walls. "This old building will burn like a stick of kindling."

Belle did not move; her face was frozen with shock.

"Please, Belle! You've got to get out of that bed!"

A rider on a fawn-colored stallion cantered along the road leading to the summit above Cripple Creek. There, he yanked his mount to a halt, and sat staring in horror at the black smoke boiling up from the town below.

Clint dug his heels into the horse and soon thundered into the yard of Jenny's cabin, leaving a cloud of dust in his wake. He bolted off the horse and ran to the door, knocking loudly, then thrust the door open. No one was home.

He slammed the door and leapt back onto his horse, racing toward Bennett Avenue. Just on the outskirts of town, he slid off the horse once more, freed him of his saddle and bridle, and with a slap on the rump to send the frightened animal running away from the danger, he plunged into the choking heat.

A woman dashed by him, gripping a baby to her breast, her face pale and tear-stained.

"Have you seen Jenny Townley?" he shouted to her.

"No," she screamed, running blindly for shelter.

People milled in groups watching in horror as the fire fighters fought the inferno. Girls who had escaped from the burning dance hall huddled together on the street corner, their clothes blackened with soot, their hair singed and hanging in their faces.

"We're out of water!" a fireman shouted.

Clint weaved his way through the frenzied crowd to the firemen.

"Can you dynamite some of those shacks up on Third?" he shouted above the din. "You might be able to divert the fire that way."

"We did that in Frisco and it worked," someone else yelled.

"Clint Kincaid!"

Joseph Townley burst through the crowd, his white shirt blackened with smoke. "Clint, you're a welcome sight," he said, throwing an arm around his shoulder.

"Reverend Townley," Clint turned to embrace him. "Where is Jenny?"

"I don't know. She was at home when I left—"

"She isn't there now," Clint interrupted, panic clutching at his jumbled thoughts.

"Reverend Townley?" A small man raced up to them, a look of terror on his face. "Belle was sick and your daughter went to see about her. Some of the people are trapped in the boarding house yonder," he pointed to the clapboard building quickly dissolving beneath relentless flames. "I don't know if your daughter got out."

Both men froze momentarily, then suddenly Clint broke through the crowd, pushing, shoving, battling his way toward the flimsy building surrounded by crimson clouds of smoke.

"No, God! Please! No!" The cry was wrenched from his soul but never escaped his parched lips until he reached the collapsing building.

"Jenny!" The name was torn from his throat as he plunged into the smoky cauldron only to be yanked back by several sooty hands.

"The building is gone," a man yelled in his ear. "If anyone is left inside it's too late."

For one split second, he hesitated, his eyes scanning the sea of faces. Jenny was not here.

"Let me go." He wrenched free, delivering several hard blows to those who held him. Then he began to cough, and in the moment that he stopped fighting, someone gave him a blow to the head. Clint fell limply, and strong arms pulled him back, a second before the greedy flames could reach him.

When Clint regained consciousness, minutes later, Joseph was lfiting his head, dabbing his sooty face with a handkerchief. "Son, we've got to be strong," Joseph was speaking as though in a daze.

Clint bolted up, his smoke-filled eyes widening in horror as he stared at the rubble heap that had once been the boarding house. Tears trickled down his dusty face.

"I think she got out, Clint." Joseph now spoke firmly. "She would have heard the shouts and left in time. We must believe that."

"But I've seen what fire and panic can do. What if the roof caved in before she got away? What if—"

"The dynamite is going to save the rest of the town," Joseph interrupted. "Once we get out of this blinding smoke, maybe we can locate her. Come on."

The two men made their way over and around rubbish to a spot away from the heat and confusion.

"I don't see her," Clint murmured, his eyes restlessly scanning the crowds of people. "If she were here I would know it—I would sense it. Oh, my sweet Jenny." He looked at Joseph with pleading eyes. "I never wrote her. She'll never know that I love her more than ever."

"The crowd is breaking up a bit," Joseph said softly. "You wait here and I'll find some of our church members. Perhaps they have seen her."

Clint slumped to the ground, then slowly raised his head. He looked first in the direction Joseph had gone, then he turned and looked behind him, in the direction of the church. Suddenly, a look of hope filled his eyes. He would go to the church. He rose to his feet and started for the structure that stood like a brave and peaceful sentinel over the turmoil below.

He broke into a run covering the path up the steep and rocky hill quickly. Then he stood solemnly beside the half-built structure, and placed a hand on its frame, almost reverently.

He looked through the open door to the altar where others had quietly gathered to pray, and stepped inside to join them.

"*Clint!*"

At the cry, several of those gathered looked up, then resumed their prayers. But Jenny was running up the aisle, her arms outstretched.

"Oh, Clint. You're here!" Tears were streaming down her face as she threw her arms around him. "I've ached for you so."

"I thought . . ." he broke off hoarsely, as he gently pushed her back to look down into her face. Jenny saw the bleak torment that still lingered in his eyes. She looked to the open door and the town below.

"The boarding house burned, didn't it?" she asked softly.

He nodded. "We heard you were there . . . ."

"With Belle," she pointed to the front of the church where the old woman sat huddled in a blanket.

"We must let your father know that you're safe. But first, I have to tell you. I thought . . ." Again he was not able to finish.

"I know what you must have thought," she said, hugging him tightly. "But I'm here with you, and we're never going to be separated again."

She leaned back to look into his face. "Let's walk outside now."

Clint nodded continuing to stare at her—at her singed hair and torn calico dress blackened with soot—as though he still could not believe she was safe.

They turned and as they hurried out of the door, something glinted on the ground and caught Jenny's eye. She knelt to retrieve a smoke-stained coin lost undoubtedly in the scurry for shelter. She rubbed the coin against her skirt and as the smoke stains vainshed, the coin gleamed brightly in her palm.

"Gold." She looked up at Clint. "It survived the fire, didn't it. Just like Maude said—when gold is tested by fire it comes out strong as ever, maybe better than it was before. I think this town has been purged as well," she sighed, staring down at the people milling helplessly among the ruins.

"We'll rebuild," Clint said, "with brick this time. The buildings will be stronger and safer."

Jenny nodded thoughtfully, gripping the coin tightly

in her hand. "Maybe we've been purged. Maybe we'll be better people too, Clint."

"I know I will, Jenny." He pulled her into his arms. "All the things we worked so hard to obtain down there are gone. Gone up in smoke while we stood watching, helpless. But the church," he glanced over his shoulder, "the church is still here." He stared down at her, his haggard eyes glowing with deeper perception, "and all of the good you and your father have done, the way you've helped people, that can never be destroyed either, can it? Jenny, I've been such a fool." He shook his head sadly.

"No, you haven't," she said, pressing her fingers to his lips. "Clint, I love you."

"Oh, Jenny, I love you too. When can we get married?"

She smiled at his almost boyish eagerness. "Well, I had hoped to be married in the church."

"Then I'd better roll up my sleeves and join the work crew, because I can't wait much longer. You see," his eyes followed a wisp of smoke into the sky, "all my false gods toppled in that fire. I'm ready now to make a commitment to you. And to God."

Arm in arm they strolled back down the hill, seeking her father to tell him the good news.

"Welcome home," Jenny whispered, and this time there would be no more goodbyes.

A Letter To Our Readers

Dear Reader:

Pioneering is an exhilarating experience, filled with opportunities for exploring new frontiers. The Zondervan Corporation is proud to be the first major publisher to launch a series of inspirational romances designed to inspire and uplift as well as to provide wholesome entertainment. In order that we might better contribute to your reading enjoyment, we would appreciate your taking a few minutes to respond to the following questions and return to:

> Anne Severance, Editor
> The Zondervan Publishing House
> 1415 Lake Drive, S.E.
> Grand Rapids, Michigan   49506

1. Did you enjoy reading KINCAID OF CRIPPLE CREEK?

  ☐ Very much. I would like to see more books by this author!
  ☐ Moderately
  ☐ I would have enjoyed it more if _____

2. Where did you purchase this book? _____

3. What influenced your decision to purchase this book?

  ☐ Cover   ☐ Back cover copy
  ☐ Title   ☐ Friends
  ☐ Publicity   ☐ Other _____

4. Please rate the following elements from 1 (poor) to 10 (superior).

☐ Heroine   ☐ Plot
☐ Hero   ☐ Inspirational theme
☐ Setting   ☐ Secondary characters

5. Which settings would you like to see in future Serenade/Saga Books?

_____ _____

_____ _____

6. What are some inspirational themes you would like to see treated in future books?

_____ _____

_____ _____

7. Would you be interested in reading other Serenade/Serenata or Serenade/Saga Books?

☐ Very interested
☐ Moderately interested
☐ Not interested

8. Please indicate your age range:

☐ Under 18   ☐ 25–34   ☐ 46–55
☐ 18–24   ☐ 35–45   ☐ Over 55

9. Would you be interested in a Serenade book club? If so, please give us your name and address:

Name _____

Occupation _____

Address _____

City _____ State _____ Zip _____

Serenade Saga Books are inspirational romances in historical settings, designed to bring you a joyful, heart-lifting reading experience.

Serenade Saga books available in your local book store:

Serenade/Serenata Books are inspirational romances in contemporary settings, designed to bring you a joyful, heart-lifting reading experience.

Other Serenade books available in your local bookstore:

#1 ON WINGS OF LOVE, Elaine L. Schulte
#2 LOVE'S SWEET PROMISE,
    Susan C. Feldhake
#3 FOR LOVE ALONE, Susan C. Feldhake
#4 LOVE'S LATE SPRING, Lydia Heermann
#5 IN COMES LOVE, Mab Graff Hoover
#6 FOUNTAIN OF LOVE, Velma S. Daniels and
    Peggy E. King.

Watch for other books in both the *Serenade Saga* and *Serenade Serenata* (contemporary) series coming soon.